The Absent City

The Absent City

Ricardo Piglia

Translated by Sergio Waisman

Duke University Press   Durham and London 2000

© 2000 Duke University Press
All rights reserved
Printed in the United States of America on acid-free paper ∞
Typeset in Carter and Cone Galliard by
Tseng Information Systems, Inc.
Library of Congress Cataloging-in-Publication Data
appear on the last printed page of this book.
Financial support for the translation provided
to Sergio Waisman by the
National Endowment for the Humanities.

The Absent City

Introduction

Sergio Waisman

The Absent City is Ricardo Piglia's third book to be translated into English, and the second published by Duke University Press. Since its original publication in Argentina in 1992, it has been widely read and hailed in the Spanish-speaking world for its combination of literary innovation and poignant sociopolitical reflection. With this translation, Duke makes available to an English-speaking audience one of the most fascinating novels to come out of Latin America in recent times.

Ricardo Piglia and His Work

Ricardo Piglia was born in Adrogué, in the Province of Buenos Aires, in 1940. His first book, a collection of short stories entitled *Jaulario* (*La invasión* in the Argentine edition), received an important prize from the Casa de las Américas in 1967. Since then, he has published three collections of short stories—*Nombre falso* (1975), *Prisión perpetua* (1988), and *Cuentos morales* (1994)—and three novels: *Respiración artificial* (1980), *La ciudad ausente* (1992), and *Plata quemada* (1997), which won the Premio Planeta that year. He has also published numerous critical articles, including three editions of the collection *Crítica y ficción* (1986, 1990, and 1993). His latest book is *Formas breves* (1999), a collection of short, critical narratives. In recent years, Piglia has also worked on several film projects. Among others, he has written the original screenplay of *Foolish Heart,* directed by

Héctor Babenco, and a screen adaptation of Juan Carlos Onetti's *El astillero*. In addition to English, his fiction and criticism have been translated into French, Portuguese, German, and Italian.

Nombre falso (*Assumed Name*), a collection of five stories and an eponymous novella, marked an important point in Piglia's trajectory and established his international importance with striking singularity. My translation of *Assumed Name* was published by the Latin American Literary Review Press in 1995. In the novella, the author himself is the protagonist attempting to solve the mystery of an unpublished manuscript allegedly written by Argentine writer Roberto Arlt. In the first part, "Homage to Roberto Arlt," fiction doubles as literary criticism as Piglia reworks a genre best exemplified by the stories of Jorge Luis Borges. The second part of the novella then produces the mysterious manuscript, "Luba."

When *Assumed Name* appeared for the first time in Argentina, Mirta Arlt, Roberto Arlt's daughter, called Ricardo Piglia on the telephone to tell him that she did not know of this story by her father, and that Piglia should not have published it without her permission. In the United States, "Luba" was cataloged by the Library of Congress with Roberto Arlt as its author, and remains miscataloged to this date. These anecdotes underscore the importance that issues of originality, translation, and recontextualization play in Piglia's work.

When Duke published Piglia's first novel, *Respiración artificial* (*Artificial Respiration*) in 1994, it brought to an English-speaking audience, in a translation by Daniel Balderston, one of the most important Latin American novels from the 1980s, and perhaps the most important one from the "dirty war" period in Argentina. *Artificial Respiration* contains many levels of ironies and double entendres, of mystery and displacements. The narrator, Renzi (a character who appears in much of Piglia's work), is searching for his uncle, who has vanished, and the search leads to a series of revealing conversations about history, exile, and literature. Written at a time when Argentina was living through the most repressive military dictatorship in its history, when thousands of citizens were "disappeared" by the government (facts not explicitly mentioned in the novel), *Artificial Respiration* displaces the focus and discusses Argentina's nineteenth-century political turmoil, including Rosas's dictatorship in the first half of that century. At a time of active censorship by the military regime, the novel has a character who is a censor trying to decipher supposedly coded letters and messages.

Plata quemada (*Burnt Money*), not yet available in English, is a fast-paced, exciting novel that revolves around the disturbing crimes of two extraordinary characters, who seek to escape the police after they rob a bank. *Burnt Money* explores the relationship between these two marginal personalities, as well as the connections between crime and community, between money and identity.

The Absent City: The Seduction of the Story

The Absent City is a captivating novel that makes use of several literary genres. On the one hand, *The Absent City* resembles a detective novel: Junior, the son of English immigrants in Argentina, is a newspaper reporter trying to solve the mystery of what is happening in the city of Buenos Aires. But it is much more than a detective novel, as, in a sense, the city becomes a metaphor for the novel, and vice versa. The world in which Junior operates is a futuristic Buenos Aires, in which the map of the city is constructed by a series of fictional narratives. The intrigue of each of these stories (written in different tones, or registers) multiplies as they intersect each other (like streets and avenues of a city) and unfold to make up the enigma of the text (the written, as well as the geographic and political text) that Junior is trying to solve.

At the heart of the novel and the city is the unusual heroine, Elena, who used to be a woman but is now a machine (she is the center of the novel and the city, since she composes the stories that make up both). Elena was Argentine writer-philosopher Macedonio Fernández's wife. In the novel, he tries to save her, when she becomes terminally ill, by placing her memories in a machine. Thus under the

3

surface there is also a story of love and loss. A man loses the woman he loves; he cannot bear that loss; therefore he builds a machine to try to preserve her memories; the machine then outlives the man. All this occurs in a city under intense police surveillance. The repressive setting reminds the reader of Argentina's deeply troubled military past, especially the period of dictatorship from 1976 to 1983.

But it also has a broader resonance with the dangers of all totalitarian regimes, and some of the twentieth-century atrocities associated with them. Thus another theme that arises is the power of language to create and define reality—the State's official version of history; a machine that creates stories that become real; the attempts of the police to control the flow of information; a world in which people tell stories in an attempt to rewrite history or to prevent others from writing it for them. The proliferation of stories in *The Absent City* becomes important as a way to challenge official versions of reality. Through a series of reproductions, translations, simulacra, and simulations, narrative becomes a site of political and aesthetic resistance.

The different genres that make up the novel—detective, love story, political or historical, science fiction—interrupt and cross each other (like the different narrative lines) to rupture the traditional form of the novel, constituting an important aspect of Piglia's innovation. More than a combination of genres, of story lines, we end up with a distorted—or, better yet, fragmented—recombination. No single genre or narrative line can contain the entire novel, and yet each one tries to tell a similar story, even as they point in different directions. For example, one might be tempted to think of *The Absent City* as a political novel, because of its specific historical references and allusions. But the text also works with a series of paranoid delusions, in which it is impossible to ever determine whether the subjects are truly the victims of a larger conspiracy or whether this belief is a product of their own minds.

Another genre that the reader might recognize is the cyberpunk version of science fiction, reminiscent of the work of William Burroughs. The interwoven stories themselves form a net—of plots,

4

characters, literary and historical references, media of communication—that seems to exist in a virtual reality, especially to the extent that they originate from a machine. A machine that produces stories; an investigation (by Junior, by the reader) that fluctuates between past, present, and future; the possibilities of artificial intelligence and neurosurgery associated with interrogations and surveillance; drug-consciousness manipulation combined with hallucinatory ambiguities—all elements that contribute to the sense of a science fiction narrative.

However, as with the other elements present in *The Absent City,* there is more than one explanation possible. The zigzagging stories told by a woman in order to seduce and survive also remind the reader of Scheherazade in *The Arabian Nights.* In other words, they touch on a tradition as old as narrative itself, the drive to tell a story, to hear a story, which speaks of the relationship between desire and storytelling, between narration and the perception of reality.

Macedonio Fernández and James Joyce

The Absent City contains references and allusions to a number of Argentine writers. In *The Absent City,* as in much of Piglia's work, there is a project to (re)draw literary genealogies and raise issues associated with accepted canons. An important aspect of a nation's identity is its literary inheritance and how this heritage is perceived—and constructed—in the present. All writers inherit a past, but, as Jorge Luis Borges might have said, they also create their precursors, by changing the way readers read previous writers through the lens of new ones.

There are also a number of references in *The Absent City* to works and writers not from Argentina: *The Arabian Nights,* Dante Alighieri, Fyodor Dostoyevsky, Robert Louis Stevenson, Edgar Allan Poe, Henry James, William Faulkner, James Joyce, and others. Of these, a few words should be said about the role of Joyce in *The Absent City.* But first, we must consider Macedonio's place in the novel.

Macedonio Fernández (1874–1952) is one of the most unusual characters in Argentine literary history, much celebrated by Borges and others for his ingenuity, and a key figure in Argentina's avantgarde movements. He married Elena de Obieta in 1901, with whom he had four children. She died in 1920. His texts include the poem "Elena Bella muerte" ("Elena beautiful death") (1920) and *No todo es Vigilia lo de los Ojos Abiertos* (*Not Everything is Wakefulness When our Eyes Are Open*) (1928). In 1904 he began writing a lifelong novel, *Museo de la Novela de la Eterna* (*Museum of the Novel of the Eternal One*). He worked on it for approximately forty-five years, until his death, but never published it. It was finally published posthumously in 1967.

In his writing, often humorous and logically unpredictable, Macedonio puts into play the importance of language in creating meaning and in our conceptions of time and space. But he does so by emptying out traditional linguistic and literary constructions and conventions to demonstrate their arbitrariness and lack of any real existence. The *Museo de la Novela de la Eterna*, a text that is both a novel and a theory of the novel, has over fifty prologues and characters with names such as Dulce-Persona (Sweet-Person), Quizágenio (Maybegenius), and the No-Existente-Caballero (Non-Existent-Knight).

But this Macedonio Fernández from history is not necessarily the Macedonio that the reader encounters in *The Absent City*. Readers should not assume that they are reading about Macedonio Fernández at a literal level. The Macedonio in *The Absent City* is not the man who lived and wrote in Argentina in the first half of the twentieth century, but rather a fictional character named Macedonio.

The origins of this narrative technique—of this inversion between the real and the fictional—in Argentine literature can be traced to Borges, whose texts actively blur the distinctions between genres: between essay and story, between literary criticism and fiction. Piglia's reworking of this technique is one way in which he dialogues textually with Borges's works and ideas. For example, the point of departure for Borges's story "Tlön, Uqbar, Orbius Tertius" is a discovery that Borges (the narrator, also a fictionalized "real" person) tells us is made by his friend Bioy Casares, whom we identify immediately as the Argentine writer, Borges's lifelong friend and literary collaborator. This is but one example of the kind of contamination between reality and fiction that Borges achieves in his work, a move that allows Borges—and Piglia as well—to interpret reality (including history, politics, and culture) through literature.

The other technique used by Borges is to have imaginary writers (such as Al-Mu'tasim in "An Approach to Al-Mu'tasim" or Herbert Quain in "Survey of the Works of Herbert Quain") invent texts to which we have access only by reading the stories in which they are described. In these stories, fictional characters write novels that are summarized for us as if they were real. Piglia's turn of the screw on this technique is to take a real character, a writer from history, and attribute to him fictional works and actions. It is the inverse, in a sense, of one aspect of Borges's poetics; and it is what he does in creating the character of Macedonio in *The Absent City*.

However, it would be misleading to imagine that the use of Macedonio's name in *The Absent City* is arbitrary. In fact, there is a move in the novel to place Macedonio's anarchic ideas as an aesthetic and political response to the totalizing narratives of the State, which seeks to order and control the individual, to determine meaning and one's place in society from outside the self. In contrast, for Macedonio, the self is not what it perceives, but what it utters. It is therefore an unstable and imaginary creation, one that resists another's definition of its existence.

Furthermore, a contrast is drawn between Macedonio's position as a writer and that of the poet Leopoldo Lugones. The novel's critique of Lugones does not necessarily relate to the value of his work, but rather to the fact that Lugones willingly allowed himself to become part of the mechanism of the State. He became the figure of the patriotic writer whom the State uses to limit freedoms. At an aesthetic level, Lugones can also be seen as the figure of the canonical writer used to exclude entry of more revolutionary or anarchistic thinkers, such as Macedonio Fernández.

The other major literary figure present in *The Absent City*, in addition to Macedonio, is James Joyce. One question that arises is why a contemporary Argentine writer such as Ricardo Piglia would turn to someone like James Joyce. I will mention just one of several possibilities here: both Joyce and Macedonio, in their respective countries and traditions, challenged the status quo aesthetically and politically. In this sense, they epitomize a certain project of the avant-garde with which Piglia clearly identifies. The question, left to the reader, is how this kind of avant-garde challenge applies to our current condition. Or, better yet, why is such a response necessary in our Neoliberal, postmodern world?

But there are other ways to approach the possible connections between Piglia, Macedonio, and Joyce. On the one hand, one can speak of certain parallels between Buenos Aires and Dublin, of their affinities in terms of their literary and historical relationships with the metropolis. On the other, at a more specific level relating to *The Absent City*, there is a way in which Junior's loss (of his daughter, when his wife abandoned him and took their daughter with her) resonates with Macedonio's loss of Elena, which leads him to build the machine in *The Absent City*, as well as Joyce's slow loss of his daughter, Lucia, who progressively lost her sanity, especially during the period in which Joyce was writing *Finnegans Wake*.

The form of the novel also draws from both Macedonio and Joyce. From Macedonio we have the idea of the novel as a museum, of a textual place in which almost anything can be made to (co)exist. And from Joyce we have the novel as city, the city as novel, composed of journeys that draw a textual map that readers can follow as they read. The configuration of the novel does not come entirely from Joyce, of course, as there is a long tradition in Argentina of textually representing the city of Buenos Aires that extends back to the nineteenth century, with writers such as Sarmiento and Echeverría, and is explored again by Borges and Arlt, and then Marechal and Cortázar, among other twentieth-century writers.

Furthermore, these various points of contact between Piglia and Joyce should provide some clues to reading "The Island," found in chapter 3 of *The Absent City*. As Piglia has explained in an interview, when writing this chapter, he asked himself: what would be the imaginary context for *Finnegans Wake?* In other words, not the context within which Joyce wrote the *Wake,* but rather the implicit reality of the text. The answer he provides is a society in which people take the *Wake* as the Book, in which language changes constantly. This invention becomes "The Island."

Finally, there is an additional parallel between the two novels that is important to mention. In a sense, what Joyce does with language in *Finnegans Wake*—cross one tongue with another, blur and distort linguistic and grammatical distinctions, to end up with a language that seems to contain all languages—is similar to what Piglia does with narrative lines in *The Absent City.* For example, there is a point in *The Absent City* when several stories cross and overlap and we find a superimposition of female narrators and different repressions. These include José Mármol's Amalia, James Joyce's Molly, Roberto Arlt's Hipólita, William Faulkner's Temple Drake (from *Sanctuary*), and Evita Perón:

> I am Amalia, if you hurry me I will say that I am Molly, I am her, locked up in the big house, desperate, pursued by Rosas's *mazorca,* I am Irish . . . , I am her and I am also the others, I was the others, I am Hipólita, the gimp, the little cripple . . . , I am Temple Drake and then, oh you despicable creatures, you made me live with a justice of the peace. . . . I remember . . . Evita slapping the ministers around, yes, she would slap the Minister of the Interior on the face the moment he uttered even the slightest derogatory comment about the working classes. (135)

Here and throughout *The Absent City,* these unexpected combinations create startling effects, a rupture with form and reality. They are meant to suggest comparisons and contrasts—literary as well as political—unachievable through traditional techniques of narration. Piglia's innovations raise questions about history and literature, and

9

our relationship to them as readers and citizens. *The Absent City* forces us to look into the face of absence—the very real absence of our contemporary world—to see and hear what we find there.

Other Literary References in *The Absent City*

Other Argentine writers, in addition to Macedonio and Borges, who appear in *The Absent City* include:

José Hernández (1834–86), a poet and politician, is the author of *Martín Fierro* (1872, 1879), the most famous epic poem of the gauchesque tradition.

José Mármol (1818–71) was a writer and politician who opposed the dictator Juan Manuel de Rosas (who ruled 1829–52). Mármol's novel *Amalia* (1852) describes the city of Buenos Aires during this period of dictatorship.

Eugenio Cambaceres (1843–88) was a writer and politician. His naturalist novels, such as *Sin rumbo* (1885) and *En la sangre* (1887), helped inaugurate the modern novel in Argentina.

Leopoldo Lugones (1874–1938) was a *Modernismo* writer, and the major literary figure in the country from the turn of the century until his death by suicide. Among others, he is the author of the novel *La guerra gaucha* (1905) and the book of poetry *Odas seculares* (1910). His political ideas evolved from socialism early in his life to an extreme nationalism with fascist undertones in his later years.

Roberto Arlt's (1900–42) novels and stories are populated by marginalized characters in urban situations. Erdosain and Hipólita, characters from *The Seven Madmen* (1929) and *The Flame-throwers* (1931), appear in *The Absent City*.

Historical References

The setting of *The Absent City* is at times ambiguous, as we are never quite sure whether we are in the past, present, or future. This effect is created, in part, through references and allusions to events from Argentina's history and geography. For example, there are some very specific references to the city and province of Buenos Aires, and to the Tigre Delta, where the Paraná and Uruguay Rivers flow into the Río de la Plata.

The most important historical allusions are to the military dictatorship that took power in March 1976 and ruled until 1983. During this period, known as the "dirty war," the government "disappeared" some thirty thousand citizens, maintaining a tight reign on all facets of society. The regime was finally forced to step down shortly after its defeat in the conflict over the Islas Malvinas with Great Britain (i.e., the Falklands War, whose British residents refer to themselves as Kelpers).

The other important allusions are to various events associated with Perón. Colonel (later General) Juan Domingo Perón rose to power in the mid-1940s, first as secretary of labor under a military regime and later as the elected president in 1946 through 1955, when another military takeover, the so-called Liberating Revolution of 1955, forced him into exile. Perón's politics are fairly difficult to describe; they can be generalized as a brand of extreme nationalistic populism, with the main support deriving from labor unions and, at times, the military. He was married to the famous Eva Duarte (Evita), who was very active in his government until her death from cancer in 1952. During Perón's exile, which lasted until 1974, the Peronist Resistance maintained a certain level of organization, planning for his eventual return. Upon Perón's return he was elected president once again and died in office in 1975. His wife of that time, Isabel, the vice-president, stepped into power until the coup of 1976.

For those interested in reading more about Argentine history, a good place to start is David Rock's *Argentina 1516–1987: From Spanish Colonization to Alfonsín* (1987).

1 THE MEETING

1

Junior always said that he liked to live in hotels because his parents were English. When he said English, he meant the nineteenth-century English travelers, the merchants and smugglers who abandoned their families to explore lands that had not yet been reached by the industrial revolution. Solitary and nearly invisible, they invented modern journalism by leaving behind their personal lives and stories. They lived in hotels and wrote their chronicles; they maintained sarcastic relationships with the local governors. That is why when his wife left him and moved to Barcelona with his daughter, Junior sold everything that was left in the house and dedicated himself to traveling. His daughter was four years old, and Junior missed her so much that he dreamt of her every night. He loved her much more than he might have imagined, and thought that his daughter was a version of himself. She was what he had been, but living as a female. To escape this image he traveled twice throughout the entire country—by train, in rented cars, in provincial buses. He stayed in boarding-houses, in buildings owned by the Rotary Club, in the houses of English consuls, and tried to look at everything through the eyes of a nineteenth-century traveler. When the money from what he had sold began to run out, he returned to Buenos Aires and went to *El Mundo* to look for work. He got a position at the newspaper and showed up one afternoon with his normal expression of astonishment on his face. Emilio Renzi took him around the offices and introduced him to his new coworkers, stuck there like prisoners. Within two months he was the editor's right-hand man, and was in charge of special investigations. By the time they realized it, he controlled all the news about the machine.

At first they thought that he worked for the police because he would publish articles before the events occurred. All he had to do was lift up the telephone and he would get the stories two hours before they happened. He was not yet thirty years old but he looked like a man of sixty: his head was shaved and he had an obsessive, typically English gaze, with small crossed eyes focused on some distant point, as if he were looking out to sea. His father, according to Renzi, had been one of those failed engineers sent from London to oversee the loading of the cattle into trains from the winter pastures of the large cattle ranches. They had lived for ten years in Zapala, at the end of the railroad lines of the Ferrocarril del Sur. Beyond that was the desert, the dust from the bones left behind in the wind from the slaughtering of the Indians. Mr. MacKensey, Junior's father, was the station master; he had a chalet with red roof tiles built just like the one where he had lived in England. The mother was a Chilean woman who left with her youngest daughter and went to live in Barcelona. Renzi learned the story when a cousin of Junior's came to look for him at the newspaper once, but for some reason the lunatic did not want to see her. The young woman was a fun-loving redhead. Renzi took her to a bar and then to a hotel that charged by the hour; at midnight he escorted her to Retiro Station and left her on the platform in front of the train. She lived in Martínez, was married to a naval engineer, and thought that her cousin was a misunderstood genius obsessed with their family's past.

Junior's father had been just like Junior: a delirious and disturbed individual who would stay up all night in Patagonia listening to shortwave transmissions of the BBC from London. He wanted to erase the traces of his personal life and live like a wild man in an unknown world hooked into the voices that reached him from his country. According to Renzi, his father's passion explained the speed with which Junior had picked up on the first defective transmissions from Macedonio's machine. "A typically British reaction," Renzi would say, "to teach a son with the example of a father who spends his life with his ear stuck to a shortwave radio." "It reminds me," Renzi said, "of the times of the Resistance, when my old man would stay up all night listening to the tapes of Perón that a contact from the Movement clandestinely brought him. They were first-generation tapes that used to slip and come unwound; they were brown and you had to put them on heads this big and then close the lid of the tape player. I remember the silence and the buzz of the tape before the recording would come in with Perón's exiled voice; he always began his speeches with 'Compañeros,' followed by a pause, as if he were leaving room for the applause. We sat around the kitchen table at midnight, engrossed like Junior's father, believing in that voice that came out of nowhere, always slower than normal, distorted somehow. It should have occurred to Perón to speak through shortwave radio. Don't you think?" Renzi asked and looked at Junior, smiling. "From Spain, in nighttime transmissions with the electrical discharges and interference, because that way his words would have arrived at the same time that he spoke them. Don't you think? Because we heard the tapes when the events had already changed and everything seemed late and out of place. I remember that every time someone talks to me about the machine's recordings," Renzi said. "It would be better if the story came straight out, the narrator should always be present. Of course I also like the idea of stories that seem to be outside time and start again every time you want them to."

They had gone down to the bar to get a sandwich after the deadlines were in. While Renzi talked about Perón's voice and the Peronist Resistance and began to tell the story of a friend of his father's, Little Monkey showed up to let Junior know that he had a telephone call. It was three in the afternoon on a Tuesday and the street lights were still on. Through the window one could see the electric lights glowing in the sun. "It looks like a movie," Little Monkey thought, "like the screen in a theater before the movie starts." He could hear what they were saying at the table as he approached, as if someone were turning up the volume on a radio.

"He was crazy—totally, totally crazy," Renzi was saying. "He'd yell 'Viva Perón!' and take on whatever came along. 'To be a Peronist, above all,' he would say, 'you have to have balls.' He could build a pipe bomb in half a minute, anywhere—in a bar, in a plaza, he'd move his little fingers like this, like a blind man. His family had a cache of arms on the corner of Martín García and Montes de Oca, so he was born playing with rods and pieces. In the Peronist Movement the guys called him Friar Luis Beltrán, and by the end everyone called him The Friar, except for a few who knew him from the beginning, from the very beginning of the mess, around '55 or '56, who called him Billy the Kid, which was the name that he had been given by Fat-Man Cooke, because just by looking at him you knew he was a young Turk, thin and delicate, you'd guess he was about fifteen or sixteen years old and already everyone and their brother was after him." Several people had gathered around Renzi at the table of the bar *Los 36 billares*. Little Monkey became distracted for a moment and stopped to listen to the story; then he made a dialing gesture in the air and Junior realized that the woman must be calling him on the telephone again. "It's her," Junior thought. "For sure." Some unknown woman had been calling him on the telephone and giving him instructions as if they were lifelong friends. The woman must have been familiar with the articles he had been publishing in the newspaper. Ever since the rumors of certain imperfections of the machine had been confirmed, a series of maniacs had begun to relay confidential information to him.

"Listen," the woman said to him. "You have to go to the Majestic Hotel, on Piedras and Av. de Mayo. Did you get that? Fuyita, a Korean, lives there. Are you going to go or not?"

"I'm going," Junior said.

"Tell him that it's me. That you spoke with me."

"Done."

"Are you Uruguayan?"

"English," Junior said.

"Come on," she said. "Don't joke around, this is serious."

The woman knew everything. She had the facts. But she mistook Junior for a friend of her husband's. Sometimes, at night, she would wake him up to tell him that she could not sleep. "It's very windy here," she would say, "they leave the window open, it feels like Siberia."

She spoke in code, with the allusive and slightly idiotic tone used by those who believe in magic and predestination. Everything meant something else; the woman lived in a kind of paranoid mystical state. Junior wrote down the name of the hotel and the information about Fuyita. "There's a woman living in a room that's an absolute dump; she's Fat-Man Saurio's girlfriend. Are you getting all this down?" she asked him. "They're going to close the Museum, so hurry. Fuyita is a gangster, they hired him as a security guard." Suddenly, it occurred to him that the woman was in an insane asylum. A madwoman who called him from Vieytes Clinic to tell him a bizarre story about a Korean gangster who was a guard at the Museum. He imagined a pay phone at the hospital. That apparatus—on the dilapidated wall, in an open passageway, in front of the bare trees in the park—was the saddest thing in the world. The woman talked constantly about the machine. She relayed information to him, told him stories. "She's connected, but she doesn't even know it. She can't free herself, she knows she has to talk to me, but she's not aware of what's happening to her." Still, he confirmed all the facts and arranged to go to the Majestic. He had to use the informants he had. He did not have too many options. He was moving in the dark. The information was very well controlled. Nobody said anything. The fact that the street lights were always on was the only thing that revealed that there was a threat. Everybody seemed to be living in parallel worlds, unconnected. "I'm the only connection," Junior thought. Everyone pretended to be a different person. Shortly before dying, Junior's father had remembered a program he had heard on a BBC transmission about psychiatry called "Science for Everyone." A doctor explained on the radio that you had to be careful when you came across a delirium of simulation; for example, that of a raving madman capable of docility, or of an idiot capable of feigning great intelligence. And his father laughed; his lungs hissed, he had difficulty breathing, but there he was, laughing. You never know if a person is intelligent or if they are an imbecile pretending to be intelligent. Junior hung up the telephone and returned to the bar. Renzi was already telling another episode from the story of his life.

"When I was a student and lived in La Plata, I earned a living teaching Spanish to right-wing Czechs, Poles, and Croats who had been expelled from their countries by the advance of history. Most of them lived in an old neighborhood in Berisso called 'The Austro-Hungarian Empire' where immigrants from Central Europe had settled since the end of the nineteenth century. They rented a room in the wood and tin tenement houses and worked in the cold-storage plants while they looked for something better. The Congress for Cultural Freedom, a support organization for Eastern European anti-Communists, protected them and did what it could to help them out. They had an agreement with the University of La Plata to hire literature students to teach them Spanish grammar. I met many pathetic cases during those years, but none as sad as Lazlo Malamüd. He had been a famous critic and professor of literature at the University of Budapest; he was the leading Central European authority on the work of José Hernández. His translation of *Martín Fierro* into Hungarian had received the annual prize of the International Association of Translators (Paris, 1949). He was a Marxist, he had belonged to the Petöfi Circle, and had survived the Nazis, but he fled in 1956 when the Russian tanks entered Hungary because he could not handle being slaughtered by those whom he had placed his hopes on. And then here, he was surrounded by the right-wing immigrants. To get away from this group he sought out intellectual circles and made himself known to them as a translator of Hernández. He could read Spanish properly, but he couldn't speak it. He had memorized all of the *Martín Fierro* and that was his basic vocabulary. He had come here in the hope of obtaining a position in the university; to get it, all he had to do was be able to teach in Spanish. They had asked him to give a lecture in the College of the Humanities, where Héctor Azeves was working; his future depended on that lecture. The date was approaching and he was paralyzed with fear. We met for the first time in mid-December; the lecture was scheduled for the fifteenth of March. I remember that I took cable car number twelve and traveled to Lazlo's dingy room in the lower part of Berisso, behind the cold-storage plant. We sat on his bed, placed a chair in front of us as a table, and began to work with the Lacau-Rosetti grammar book. The university paid me ten pesos per month, and I had to keep a kind of record with Malamüd's signature to confirm the attendance. I would see him three times a week. He talked to me in an imaginary language, full of guttural *r*'s and gaucho-like interjections. He tried to explain to me in a gabble the desperate feeling of being condemned to expressing himself like a three-year-old child. The imminence of the lecture had him plunged into such a panic that he could not go beyond the first-conjugation verbs. He was so dejected that one afternoon, after a very long silence, I offered to read whatever he wanted to say in his place; then poor Lazlo Malamüd let out a screeching laugh to let me know that in spite of the desperate situation he had not lost his sense of the ridiculous. How was I to read his lecture if he was the one who had to teach?

" 'I no worrk then die of this estrra-orrdinary suffer-ring,' he said.

"It was funny, it's funny to see someone who doesn't know how to speak your language try to express himself with words. One afternoon, I found him sitting down, facing the window, without any strength left, ready to give up.

" 'No more, no,' he said. 'An infamy my life. I don't deserrve all this a-humiliation. First I becoming angr-ry then the melancholy. Eyes sprring tearrs that don't alleviate their suffer-ring.'

"I always thought that that man, trying to express himself in a language of which he only knew its greatest poem, was a perfect metaphor for Macedonio's machine. Telling everyone's story with lost words, narrating in a foreign tongue. See? They gave me this," he said to Junior and showed him a cassette tape. "A very strange account.

The story of a man who does not have words to name the horror. Some say that it's fake, others say it's the pure truth. The inflections of speech, a harsh document, directly from reality. There are many copies throughout the city. They make them in Avellaneda, in clandestine labs out in the province, in the cellars of the Mercado del Plata, in the subway at Nueve de Julio. They say that they're fake, but that's not going to stop it." Renzi was laughing. "If the Argentine novel, the patriotic verse, started with Cambaceres, then that's what you have to write about, Junior—what are you waiting for?"

"There's a woman," Junior said. "She calls me on the telephone, passes information on to me. Now she says I should go to a hotel, the Majestic on Piedras and Av. de Mayo. There's a guy there, a certain Fuyita, a Korean who works in the Museum, a security guard, the night watchman. I don't know, maybe she works for the police."

"In this country, everyone who's not in jail works for the police," Renzi said, "including the thieves."

Junior stood up. He was leaving.

"Did I give you the recording?" Renzi asked. "Here," he said, and handed him a cassette tape. "Listen to it, then you can fill me in."

"Perfect."

"I'll meet you here, tomorrow."

"At six," Junior said.

"Be careful."

"Yeah."

"It's full of Japanese out there," Renzi said.

Outside, the cars were coming and going. "They are always watching, even if there is no point to it," Junior thought. The sky was gray; at 3:50 P.M. the president's helicopter flew over the avenue toward the river. Junior checked the time and entered the subway. Toward Plaza de Mayo. He leaned back against the window, half asleep, letting the swaying train move him around. They look at each other, the dumbshits, they travel underground just for that. An old woman traveled standing up, her face swollen from so much crying. Simple people, proletariats dressed to go out, modern clothes from Taiwan.

Couples holding hands, checking out their reflections in the window. The dark ones with black hair, the Peronios, as Renzi called them. "In the middle of everyone they shaved me clean like a nobody," Junior sang to himself. "I'm mute. I sing with my thoughts. The barber, an Italian immigrant on Av. Constitución, didn't want to do it at first. 'What are you trying to do, kid?' I don't want lice," Junior had answered. He shined his white bowl with brilliantine ("I don't want lice"). Miguel MacKensey (Junior), an English traveler. The lighted subway sped through the tunnel at eighty kilometers per hour.

2

The Majestic Hotel, with its marble entrance and dilapidated walls, was right on the corner of Piedras and Av. de Mayo. In the mezzanine at the top of the stairs there was a desk, and behind it an old man petting a roan cat, his face next to its nose. Junior saw a carpeted hallway, several closed doors, and the entrance to a basement. He stopped warily and lit a cigarette.

"This animal that you see right here," the old man said without looking up, "is fifteen years old. Do you know how old that is for a cat?" He dragged his words as he spoke, with an intonation somewhere between respectful and cunning, his thin neck buried in the lustring lapels of a corduroy jacket. He was standing between the key rack and a glass door, and held the cat on the counter. The bow-legged animal began to move slowly, arching its back. "This animal is a miracle of nature. He understands as if he was a person. I brought him from out in the country and he has stayed here ever since. A gaucho cat." When he smiled his small eyes became smaller. "From Entre Ríos."

Junior leaned over the cat, who breathed with a kind of quivering, and petted it on the back.

"He's nervous, see? He understands everything, he doesn't like the smell of tobacco. Can you feel how he breathes?"

"My name is Junior," he said. "I need to see Fuyita."

"And?" the old man asked with his little suspicious smile.

"Do you know if he is in?"

"Mr. Fuyita? I couldn't say. You'll have to speak with the manager."

"Nice cat," Junior said and grabbed the cat by its nape with a quick move. He pressed him against the counter. The cat shrieked, terrified.

"What are you doing?" the old man asked, covering his face with his hand to protect himself.

"Give me the number," Junior said. "I work in the circus."

The old man had fallen back against the wall and was looking at Junior as if he wanted to hypnotize him. His eyes were two small quail eggs in his wrinkled face.

"That animal is the only thing I have in the world," the old man begged, "don't hurt him."

Junior released the cat, who jumped and left, meowing like a baby; then he took out a 1,000 pesos bill folded in half.

"I need the room number."

The old man tried to smile, but he was so nervous that he just stuck the tip of his tongue out. "An iguana," Junior thought. He reached for the bill and put it in the small front pocket of his jacket with a furtive move.

"Two twenty-three. Room two twenty-three. Fuyita is Christ," he said. "They call him Christ, get my drift?" He stuck his tongue out twice and turned around toward the key rack. "Go on up," he said. "I'm not here, you didn't see me." He was sticking his tongue out and in, facing the wall so that no one would see him.

The elevator was a cage, its ceiling full of inscriptions and graffiti. "Language kills," Junior read. "Viva Lucia Joyce." He looked at his face in the mirror; it looked as if he were trapped in a spider web— the shadow from the wall's gratings covering his shaved cranium, his melancholic skull. The hallway on the second floor was empty. The yellow walls and the carpets drowned out the harsh rumblings from the street. Junior rang room two twenty-three. The buzzer seemed to ring somewhere else, outside the hotel, outside the city even.

"What is it?" a woman's voice said after a while.

"Fuyita," he said.

The woman opened the door just a crack. Junior thought that maybe Fuyita was not a man. "Fuyita Coke, the Japanese Dame."

"You're Fuyita," he said.

The woman laughed.

"Language kills," he quoted blindly. The woman was a pale outline in the room's semi-darkness.

"Who are you? Did the Deaf Girl send you?" she murmured. Then she raised her voice: "Say, why don't you go to hell? Who in the world are you?" There was a brief hesitation, a deep breath. "He's not here."

"Calm down," Junior said. "My name is Junior."

"Who?" she said.

"Junior," Junior said, pushing at the door. It opened gently, without any resistance from the woman.

"Asshole," she said. "Get out of here, you son of a bitch."

She spoke in a low voice, as if she were shouting in a dream.

The room was dimly lit and the air smelled of camphor and alcohol and cheap perfume. The woman headed back toward the bed. Junior followed her slowly, trying not to lose track of her in the thick shadows cast by the furniture.

"You better not touch me or I'll scream," she said. "If you touch me I'll scream."

He finally became accustomed to the greenish light in the room and was able to see her face. She had been a blond, she had been hit, her lips were swollen, her mouth cracked, her skin full of welts. She wore a shirt that barely covered her breasts and a man's pair of shoes without shoelaces.

"Why did he hit you?" he asked.

The woman dragged her feet as she walked. She sat down on the bed and rested her elbows on her knees absentmindedly.

"And who are you?" she asked.

"I'm going to help you."

"Yeah, sure," she said. "Did Fuyita send you? Are you Japanese? Come here, let me see."

She lit a cigarette lighter. The flame illuminated the mirror on the dresser.

"I came to see him," Junior said. "He told me to meet him here."

"He left. He's not coming back. Poor guy." She started crying without making any noise. Then she leaned down and looked around for her bottle of gin. She was not wearing anything other than the shirt and you could see her breasts, she did not try to cover herself up. "Shit," she said, tilting the empty bottle. "He can die for all I care." She made an effort to smile. "Be good and go buy me some more."

"In a moment. First we'll talk, then I'll go and get you some gin. Turn on a light—"

"No," she cut him short. "What for? Keep it as it is. Give me a cigarette."

Junior handed her the pack. She opened it avidly and started smoking.

"Tell me if he isn't rotten? He took my clothes so I wouldn't go out. What did he think? That I was going to run after him?"

"He left," Junior said. "He put your clothes in a suitcase and left. Fuyita Coke. Do you want some?"

"I don't do coke," she said. "It's been years. Do you come from La Plata? Are you a narc? It's Deaf Girl's fault, she's a mare, a drug addict. I'm sure he's with her." She leaned forward to speak to him in a low voice. Up close her face looked as if it were made of glass. "He wants to leave me for that shrew. Leave me for that bitch." She stood up and started moving around the room. "After I . . . do you know what I did for him, what I did for that man?" She stopped to one side, in front of the chair where he had sat down. "If you could see what's become of me," she said, and lifted her shirt to show him her legs, and brought her feet—in the rubber-soled shoes—together. "Don't you see? I danced in the Club Maipo, I did. I'd come down completely naked, wearing feathers. Ms. Joyce. It means happiness. I sang in English. What does she think, that nobody? I've been lead dancer since I was sixteen and now that bitch comes and takes him from me." Junior figured that the woman was going to start crying. "He decided to send me to Entre Ríos, can you understand that? He says that I'm too stifled here. But do you understand what he wants to do to me, that he wants to bury me alive?" Desperation made her move in place and breathe heavily. "What would I do if he sent me to Entre Ríos? What would I do there, answer me that?"

"The countryside is pretty," Junior said. "You could raise animals, live near nature. Ninety percent of the gauchos just fuck the sheep."

"What are you saying, you degenerate? Are you sick? Why did they shave your head? Are you Russian? I saw a movie once with a Russian whose head looked like a bowl, just like yours. Did you have ringworm? Are you from the country?"

"Yes," Junior said. "From the town of Gualeguay. My old man is the foreman at the Larrea cattle ranch. He was, that is. A drunk worker killed him, betrayed him, stabbed him with a knife when he was getting out of a sulky."

"And then?" the woman asked. "Go on."

"That's all," Junior said. "He had it in for him because my father had called him a bum at a dance once. He waited for his chance and finally paid him back. They're all drug addicts, out in the country. Always hallucinating."

"Yes," she said. "That's what I'm saying. I can't sleep out in the country. Wherever you look there are drugs and trash."

She walked toward an old armoire with a crescent-shaped mirror in the rear of the room. Junior managed to see the reflection from the mirror that broke the semi-darkness when she opened the armoire, then a mattress that was rolled up and tied with wire, and an empty hanger. The woman stood on her toes and searched the upper shelves. From behind she seemed very young, almost a girl. When she turned around she had a bottle of perfume in her hand. English Cologne La Franco. She opened it and took a drink, raising her face toward the ceiling. She wiped her mouth and looked at him again.

"What's wrong?" she said.

"Another thing about the country," Junior said, "are the locusts.

Short-horned grasshoppers. You have to make noise so they won't land, horns, shots, my father would even blow the siren on the boat. Or else with smoke, burn the cane thickets, the dry grass. That's why I like the city—no locusts. Just mosquitoes and cats."

The woman left the armoire open and walked toward the center of the room with the bottle of perfume pressed against her stomach. She moved slowly and looked at Junior with a suspicious expression on her face.

"And why was it that you wanted to see him?"

"I have something to ask him."

"He told you to meet him here? If you want to see him, why don't you go look for him at the Museum? Tell me, you wouldn't be a friend of Fat-Man Saurio's?"

"Calm down, shhh . . . ," Junior said. "Silence in the night. Fuyita asked me to come here. Now . . . if you say that he's in the Museum."

"Me?" The woman started to laugh nervously. "What did I say, kid?" She lifted the bottle of perfume and took another drink. Then she put a few drops on her fingertips and patted herself behind the ears. Junior could smell the perfume's mild fragrance mixed with the closed-in smell of the room.

"Maybe he's in the Museum, maybe he's not. If you're such good friends with Fat-Man Saurio, you must know something. Why don't you have him tell you about Deaf Girl." She started to laugh again, as if she were coughing. "Tell me the truth, is he with her or not?"

She had started to cry and could not stop. She pressed her closed fists against her eyes. Junior felt sorry for the woman and asked her not to cry.

"How can you ask me not to cry, do you want to tell me that? With what he's done to me!"

"Here, take this," he said, and handed her a handkerchief. "Calm down, don't cry. Where are you from?"

"From here, I've always lived in the hotel, I'm the girl from the Majestic. But I come from far away, from the interior of the country, from the south. From Río Negro. Look, I stained it all," she said, and tried to fold the handkerchief, smiling. "Do you think it'll show?" She was touching her bruises with her fingertips.

"No," he said. "No. But why don't you clean yourself up a little. Come here, let me see."

He moistened the handkerchief with the eau de cologne and cleaned her bruised face, which she allowed him to do with her eyes closed.

"That's enough," she said. "That's enough. Hold on, let me turn on a light." She went up to a lamp with a pleated ruffle lampshade. It gave off a bluish light when she switched it on. Then she looked at herself in the mirror. "Mother of God, I look like a monster." She began to fix her hair. She looked at one of her legs. "Anyway, I'm full of wounds and it doesn't hurt, I don't feel much, see?" She lifted her shirt and showed him the scars. "This was done by a motorcycle, this by a dog that bit me, here I sort of ran into a wall, I didn't see it. But it doesn't hurt. Most complain about every little bruise. I've been knocked around by that brute. People are afraid of pain, but not me, right now I don't feel it at all. It has to do with endorphins."

"With what?" Junior asked.

"*Endorphins.* It's scientific, kid, they explained it to me at the clinic. It's a natural sedative made by the body. If you do heroin, the body quits making endorphins. Just stops. That's why when you quit everything hurts, because you don't have enough endorphins. In my case, I think it made too much and things don't hurt like they should. That's why I drink, anyway. Alcohol. Out in the province there's a lot of heroin, in the country, in the valley, everyone can get it, they carry it on the sulkies, the Italian farmers hide it in their boots."

"Do you have any now?"

"Never. I don't buy it, I left that shit behind. When you're on horse you don't feel anything. Anyway, your body changes—you don't shower for a week but you don't stink because you don't secrete anything. You don't cry, you don't pee, you don't feel cold or hot, you barely eat. You can be a heroin addict your whole life, they know that you don't die from it, unless it's of very poor quality, the worst of the worst, which would poison you. But you have to be a millionaire to afford pure heroin. And one thing's for sure: the day you skip a dose, the withdrawal symptoms kill you."

"You can't quit."

"What do you mean you can't quit? You're crazy. You have to go somewhere where there isn't any, where you can't get it even if you're dying. I left the small town, where they sell it even in kiosks, and came to the capital, and locked myself in a bathroom for three days. When you quit heroin everything is reversed. You sweat a lot, I was always all sweaty, they'd lift me from the tiles and I'd be totally wet. It's terrible, because you're supernervous and lethargic at the same time. Besides, you cry over anything. I'd look at an ashtray and cry. I started drinking then. At first, I remember, I drank Ocho Hermanos Anisette."

"It's better."

"It's the same shit. In order not to be an alcoholic you have to avoid drinking by yourself. Now I wake up in the middle of the night, drink a little bit of gin and go back to sleep."

Junior looked at the woman, who was touching up her face. Her skin was taut and shiny as if it were made out of metal.

"Come here," he said. "I want you to look at this picture."

It was a snapshot of a young woman wearing a plaid skirt and a black turtleneck sweater.

"And who is this?" she said, grabbing the picture with both hands.

"Have you ever seen her?"

The woman shook her head no.

"Did they take her away?"

"She died," he said.

"Who did her in? Fuyita?"

"Do you think he did it?"

"Me? Are you crazy, kid? I don't know anything." She leaned over on the bed and started filing her nails. "Don't pay any attention to me. You better watch out, too, because I'm half-crazy. And who knows this little cutie, anyway?" She raised her face. "Deaf Girl is always running around with women. Have you been to the Museum yet?

28

There's a machine, do you know or not? There's something very strange in all of that."

"Nyet."

"Everything is *scientific*. Nothing evil. I met a Russian guy once who had invented a metal bird that could predict rain. This is the same. Pure science, no religion."

"No," Junior said. "Is the machine a woman?"

"She *used* to be a woman."

"They locked her up."

"She was in a clinic for a year. Don't tell him I told you because he'll kill you, Fuyita will. Don't let him know you came here. He's jealous as a snake."

"In the country I used to kill them with a pitchfork. Like this," Junior said, and made the motion of stabbing something on the floor. "The small snakes. Is your name Elena?"

"Not mine, hers. I'm Lucia. I used to live in Uruguay, I sang in the Club Sodre, that should tell you everything. That's where I first saw her, they used to display her in a dance hall behind glass. She was full of tubes and cables. All white."

"Is she in the Museum?"

"Yes. Fuyita fell in love with the machine, and I've lost him, I know it. She lives in the Museum. He thinks that in Entre Ríos I'm not going to find out, but they know about her everywhere in the country. He always loved me, he did. He gets angry because he's desperate."

Through the window could be heard the soft echo of a song that was lost in the rumble of the city.

"*You and I, who loved each other so much,*" Lucia sang. "*We must go our separate ways . . . you and I.*"

She looked like a girl, she must have been thirty years old but it seemed as if she had never aged.

"You sing well," he said, and stood up. "You should take care of yourself."

"What?" she asked. "Are you leaving already?"

"I'm leaving."

29

"Aren't you going to bring me the gin?"

"Yes."

The woman shook her head as if to wake up and tried to smile.

"Gin, and if you can, some bread."

"Okay," he said.

"Bread, some salami, anything."

"Okay, gin and something to eat," Junior said. He walked to the door followed by the woman, limping behind him.

"I'll be right back."

He opened the door and went out to the hallway. It was still empty, illuminated by a pair of bare bulbs hanging from the ceiling.

"Listen," she said.

Junior turned around. The woman was standing behind him, grabbing the door and holding her shirt closed across her chest with one hand to cover herself from the cold.

"Bring whatever you can find, a little can of pâté, whatever they have."

"Okay," he said. "Yes."

Outside, night had fallen. Junior hailed a taxi and asked the driver to take him to the Museum. It was more than an hour away. The ride was smooth. It was growing dark and the whole city was illuminated. He put on his headphones. Crime and the City Solution was playing. Somewhere from the rooftops searchlights swept across the sky with blue beams. He had the recording that Renzi had given him. It was the machine's latest known narration. A testimony, the voice of a witness recounting what he had seen. The events occurred in the present, on the edge of the world, the signs of horror marked on the earth. The story circulated in the form of copies and reproductions from hand to hand. It was available in the bookstores on Av. Corrientes and in the bars of the Bajo, the neighborhood near the port. Junior put in the cassette tape and let himself be carried away by the inflections of the person who began to narrate. Beside him, the city dissolved in the fog of autumn while the taxi turned down Av. Leandro Alem, heading south.

The Recording

The first Argentine anarchist was a gaucho from Entre Ríos. He met Enrico Malatesta once in some fields near the town of Bragado when a great flood brought them together. They spent three days sheltered on the roof of a church, covered by the Italian man's raincoat, watching the water rise and the floating branches and dead animals brought in by the Paraguay River. Curled up beneath the spread-out coat, they ate wet crackers and drank gin until the rain subsided. During those days, speaking in a kind of pidgin Spanish mixed with Italian, aided by small drawings and signs, Malatesta convinced the gaucho of the truths of anarchism. Aha, the peasant would say, aha. And he'd agree by nodding his head. That gaucho was Juan Arias. He traveled around to the large cattle ranches preaching the Idea he had learned from Malatesta until he was killed by a group of murderers from the Nationalist Autonomist Party. They pressed him up against the atrium of a church on an election day, on a Sunday, and stabbed him to death because he claimed that the oral vote was unfair to the poor and humble in the countryside. Out in the province they called him The Other Fierro because when he didn't know how to convince people and he ran out of words he'd start reciting Hernández's poem. The gauchos speak in verse and the workers stutter. The Stutterer, everyone knows him, thin, jumpy eyes, evasive gaze. In the world of labor, in the factories, people don't speak like this, suddenly, all at once. The worker's words, the worker's words sound like babble, a stuttering that struggles to express itself. This can be seen clearly on television when people from the work-world are asked to say something in an interview, for example. You have to give them at least five or six minutes more than others, because their words are broken up with silences, except in the case of the union representatives who speak like radio announcers and can come up with phrases right on the spot. It's a manner of speech that I know very well. Say your line, say your line, tell your story, and the man has difficulties telling his story and saying his line, it's a tragedy. Even my mother, before she died, told me of a peasant who was executed in a plaza, tied to a pole. She was never able to forget that man, a short foreigner, because the town's loudspeakers kept playing music and advertisements while they shot him, as if nothing was happening. I've seen things that make me want to start life over again, without any memories. I've been on the verge of leaving my wife and children, of taking a train, of going to Lomas, to my sister's house in Bernal, to Chivilcoy, to Bolívar. But it's no use, if you leave, your memories still go with you. They killed them like sparrows, running, hooded, what can a person do, their hands tied, they would shoot them from only two meters away and throw them in the pits, then they would come with bulldozers and cover the graves, sometimes they even made the wretches shovel the ditch themselves before killing them. You would see them as if in a dream, the naked Christians digging the hole. Around those times I found myself working with a gentleman named Maradey, Maneco Maradey. The field is located on the other side of the forest, I always called it "Las Lomitas," a field of two, three thousand hectares, that stretched as far as La Calera, El Diquecito, La Mezquita. I took care of the animals, we planted a few things, I'd get a certain percentage from the animals when they were sold instead of a fixed salary. I worked there with that gentleman the entire month of April, and there were some abnormalities in those fields, at the very, very back of it all, armed men, beyond the gate, some barracks, a large shed rather, located on the double highway to Carlos Paz, the highway wasn't open then, there was a road called El Camino Viejo a La Calera that was intersected by a paved road, south of Malagüeño, no, north of Malagüeño, I'm sorry, I had a dairy farm some five hundred meters from that shack, my wife and I were cleaning the jars when the incident with the calf took place. It turns out that in the cornfield, right out there, there was a pit, and my calf fell into it, you see, a pit, exactly eighteen meters long. I'll explain to you why it was exactly eighteen meters long, because the calf falls into the pit, it was arched like this, from higher to lower, you couldn't see anything from outside, the calf was bleating inside and outside a cow was scraping at the ground, like this, with its hoof, it was mooing, calling the calf. And so I go and ask this friend, Maradey, who was just about to leave in his truck, to lend me some boards because one of my calves has fallen into a pit, into a pit from a mill I thought at first, no? Then I go with two workers to bring some large horses, some percherons, and I go to Malagüeño and ask for exactly forty meters of rope, and they give me just about forty meters of rope. Okay, so we put the boards like this until we start shining some light down with some mirrors to try to find the calf, and we see, how can I tell you? This man, Maradey, he didn't care, nothing bothered him, that image, no one can imagine it, what was in that pit, those corpses, and the man and I put together a harness with that rope, and then, lighting my way with the mirrors, I bend the rope in half and grabbed it in the middle, I make a lasso on one end and I send it down. The small calf was standing, it was a black calf, kind of thin, tall, its legs sticking straight down, and as I was lowering the rope— looking through the mirror—there were all sorts of terrible things in there, bodies piled up, remains, even a woman all rolled up, sitting like this, her arms across her legs, hunched over, you could tell she was young, that woman, her head sunk into her chest, her hair hanging down, barefoot, her pants rolled up, and above her there seemed to be another person, I thought it was also a woman, fallen with her hair forward, her arms twisted backward like this, it seemed, I don't know, it was like a dug-up graveyard, the effect of what was in there, in the mirror, the light it gave off, like a circle, I would move it and see the pit, in that mirror, the shimmering remains, the light would reflect inside and I saw the bodies, I saw the earth, the corpses. Then, in the mirror, I saw the light and the woman sitting and in the middle, the calf, there it was, its four legs stuck in the mud, stiff with fear, and when we started pulling it out we noticed that it had broken its right leg up almost near its back, above the shoulder blade, and we pulled it out, poor little guy, its eyes looked almost human. I remember that I hosed it off and that I was getting my face wet with the water so that Maradey wouldn't notice that I was crying, and I could barely breathe and I ask him what are we going to do, and he says, nothing, leave everything and not say anything. And I never went back, I don't think, I sort of left my house to live with Old-Man Monti because I didn't want my daughters to do any of those things that young people do, I didn't want them to dance, nor have a good time, I couldn't listen to the radio, so since I was so bothersome to everyone I left, I made myself a bed at the cattle station, at the edge of the field, and I was more comfortable there, with Don Monti, I could think, he had seen everything, he had been jailed by the conservatives before. There has never been anything like this, he tells me. He once saw a man killed by the police in Puente Barracas just to teach people a lesson, they put him up against a back wall, a large man, they held him by his hair like this and killed him, you see, Don Monti says. But this, he said. This is like Dante's *Inferno,* he says. I remember that Old-man Monti was having a smoke when I told him, he was a man who could handle anything, he had worked in the capital and then moved to the interior when his wife and kids died in a fire. He was the first one to tell me what was going on with the frost. Because we were just above it, on this side of the fence, the small dairy, on this side of the large prairie, the only area with grass, because El Torito Hill, what is known as El Torito Hill, is all natural fields with rocks and prairies full of grazing pastures, the ruminants really seek it out, and that area isn't cultivated, nothing was done there in those days. I could see the whole field from up there, the entire prairie, the only one with green grass and soft earth that could be cultivated, you see, and below, the pits, I never put a cross out there, nothing. Sometimes you'd see the carrion hawks flying over, they couldn't cover everything up. They were digging and digging, as the winter approached you'd see more. They did everything at night and in the morning, with the frost, the squares, the white horror. On some pits you could tell they had thrown in slaked lime, the lime always rose to the surface, the grass doesn't grow quickly enough and then with the frost, the field gets frost burn when it freezes, it gets frost burn. I mean, you can see the whole wide plains with those white rectangles, one almost right next to the other, sometimes they left five or six meters in between, you could see rocks that they couldn't dig out, sometimes they would start a pit and sixty centimeters down they'd hit a large stone, so they'd dig right next to it, sometimes they'd make the pits a little thinner, sometimes a little larger, the pits were two by three meters in size, or something like that, and the earth, when they covered them up there was a lot of earth left over, the pits never ended up even, some were parallel to each other, but they were almost everywhere, the pits, because sometimes they would come to dig them on one side, then on another, and there was always so much earth left over, always so much left over, they would dig at night, even when it rained, they didn't know what to do with the remains. It was an unmeasurable map of crowded pits in that large prairie, that's what I say. I couldn't tell you how many, but I figure easily over seven hundred, seven hundred and fifty, I figure, because that area had possibly sixteen hectares, fifteen or sixteen, it's hard to tell, and it was almost completely covered, a cemetery without crosses, nothing, completely wild. There were even some pits that would go unused for six or seven days. During the day, I climbed down into several of these pits, before anyone had been buried in them, during the day all you can see is the field and the pits, the field and the pits, I even rescued some small dogs once, and a few hares that used to fall in, too. Those pits came up above my head, maybe they were more than two meters deep, and sometimes, by the following evening, they were no longer there, sometimes you could hear everything through the window, you'd see lights, movement, lanterns, armed men. And sitting with Monti on the small low chairs in the patio facing the plains, thinking I have to get out of here, but how could I have left, where to, in those times? I thought I'd go to the Chaco area where I had a buddy, but it would be worse wherever I went, I wouldn't have been able to say anything, at least there I was with Don Monti, we're the last ones, I thought, we took care of the dairy farm, of the animals, we waited for the winter to pass sitting at the door of the ranch, Don Monti would raise his hand, like this, I remember, and he'd say they come from there and from there, they would back the truck in and kill what they had brought, everything that they brought, the people with their hands tied, in hoods, right there, what could they do? Without even turning the car radio off, a car without a license plate, with music and commercials, huh, Don Monti, sitting at the door of the ranch, at the cattle station. That's how it is, the old man would say to me, worse than animals, the worst of the worst. Then he'd stop talking, take a drag from his cigarette, raise his hand, show me the prairies, below.

"You know," he says to me, "this is the map of hell." The ground was a map, what I'm telling you here, it's true, it was a map, I mean, of unmarked graves, with frost-burned sections like slabs of stone and then earth or grass. It can only be covered over so much because in the long run the frost burn, the dug-up earth, can be seen, but of course the harm has already been done by then. Because at times when they knew that there was a mound of rocks underneath they would try to joist them out, there were even some long trenches out there, they would dig until they hit some stones and then they would just stop, see? That's what you'd see, in the winter, out in the large prairie of Las Lomitas. The grass had been burned by the frost and you could see all the pits, especially the ones with slaked lime, you could see them everywhere, ones of this shape, others lengthwise, you could see very large numbers of them, let me tell you. A map of graves like we see in these mosaics, like this, that was the map, it looked like a map, after the frost, the earth, black and white, a map of hell.

II THE MUSEUM

The Museum was in a remote part of the city, near the park and behind the Congress Building. To get to the round hall where the machine was exhibited you had to go up a ramp and along a corridor with acrylic walls. You could see her at the end of the hall, standing on a black platform. Diagrams, photographs, and copies of the texts were mounted along the walls. Junior jotted down a few items in his notepad as he walked through the gallery following the history displayed in the glass cases.

At first they had tried to make a machine that could translate texts. This was a fairly simple system; it looked like a phonograph with all sorts of cables and magnets inside a glass box. One afternoon they fed it Poe's "William Wilson" and asked it to translate it. Three hours later the teletype began to print the final version. The story was stretched out and modified to such a degree that it was unrecognizable. It was now called "Stephen Stevensen." That was the first story. In spite of its imperfections, everything that followed was already synthesized in that first story. The first work, Macedonio had said, anticipates all those that come after it. We had wanted a machine that could translate; we got a machine that transforms stories. It took the theme of the double and translated it. It makes due as well as it can. It takes what is available and transforms what appears to be lost into something else. That is life. Macedonio was fifty years old at this point. He did not want to sell the patent because there was nothing to sell. He had intended to perfect the apparatus (as he called it) with the intention of entertaining people in small towns out in the country. I think it is an invention that will be more entertaining than radio, he used to say, but it is still too early to call it a success. He admonished prudence and refused to accept any form of support from the government. He was going to give a lecture at the university to explain the scope of the invention. ("It's part of 'The Ohno?' series," Macedonio said. "What are 'The Ohno?'? They are devices that no one ever believes will work until they are seen in full operation.") Everything had gone very well. Better than expected. The machine had grasped the form of Poe's narration and proceeded to change the anecdote. The next thing they had to do, therefore, was program it with a variable set of narrative nuclei, and let it go to work. The key, Macedonio said, is that it learns as it narrates. Learning means that it remembers what it has already done, it accumulates experience as it goes along. It will not necessarily make better stories each time, but it will know the stories it has already made, and perhaps give them a plot to tie them all together at the end. He thought it would be an extremely useful invention because there were very few old men left to tell ghost stories in the countryside at night. The last one I knew lived in Coronel Vidal; the guy who told the story about the invisible gaucho, Macedonio said. He came up with it all by himself, out of nowhere, perfecting it with time, drinking *mate* out in the country, the strong winds of the prairie blowing in his face. A cousin of mine once wrote to tell me that someone had told him the very same story in Spain. And the same story also appeared among a group of sailors in the Canary Islands, on Tenerife Isle. But the person who lived it was Don Sosa, a cattle herder who ended up paralyzed from jumping in the water so many times to rescue lost calves when he worked in the Echegoyen cattle ranches near Quequén. Here is the story.

The Invisible Gaucho

Burgos was a short cattle herder of Indian descent who was hired in Chacabuco to help drive a herd of cattle to Entre Ríos. They left at dawn, but were hit by a storm when they were only a few leagues out. Burgos worked with the others to keep the cattle from running off. Toward the end, he saved a lost calf that had gotten stuck in the mud, its legs spread out in the wind and rain. He hoisted it up without getting off his horse and placed it across his saddle. The animal struggled. Burgos held it with just one hand and rode over to release it with the rest of the herd. He did it to show off his skills, as if he thought the move would earn him the respect of his companions. But he regretted it at once because none of the other men looked at him, nor did anyone make the least comment. He put the incident out of his mind, but he began to get the strange feeling that the others had something against him. They only spoke to him when they were giving orders, and they never included him in their conversations. At night he was the first to go to sleep, and he would see them from under his blankets laughing and telling jokes near the fire. He felt he was living a nightmare. He had never been in a situation like this in the sixteen years of his life. He had been mistreated, but never forgotten and ignored. The first stop was in Azul, where they arrived late on a Saturday afternoon. The leader said they would spend the night in town and leave the next day at noon. They put the cattle in a small yard, which everyone called the church corral, close to where the town ended and the plains began. It was said that a chapel once stood there that had been destroyed by the Indians in the Great Indian Raid of 1867. There were a few low walls left that served to keep the cattle inside the corral. Burgos thought he saw the shape of a cross formed by the bricks where some weeds grew. It was a hole of light in the wall, drawn by the sunlight. Enthusiastic, he showed it to the others, but they walked right on past as if they had not heard him. The cross could be seen clearly in the air as the sun set. Burgos kissed his fingers and crossed himself. There was dancing in the general store. Burgos sat at a table apart from everyone else. He saw the men laughing together and getting drunk. He saw them head to the back room with the women who were sitting in a line at the counter, and would have liked to pick one out for himself as well, but he was afraid of being ignored, so he stayed where he was. Still, he imagined picking out the attractive blond in front of him. She was tall and seemed to be the oldest of the group. He would take her to the room, and when they were lying in bed, he would explain what was happening to him. The woman wore a silver cross that hung between her breasts and spun it around while Burgos told her the story. Men like to see others suffer, the woman said, they looked at Christ because they were drawn by his suffering. She spoke with a foreign accent. If the story of the Passion weren't so horrendous, the woman said, no one would have bothered to look after the Son of God. Burgos heard the woman saying this to him and got up to ask her to dance, but he thought that she would not see him, so he pretended he had gotten up to order a gin. That night the men did not go to sleep until dawn, and everyone slept well into the morning. Around noon they started to herd the cattle out of the corral toward the road. The sky was dark and Burgos did not see the cross in the church wall. They galloped in the direction of the storm, where the low clouds blended into the broad fields. A little later raindrops as heavy as twenty-cent pieces began to fall. Burgos covered himself with his watertight poncho and rode in front of the herd. He knew how to do his job, and they knew that he knew how to do his job. This was the only bit of pride left in him, now that he was less than nothing. The storm grew worse. They drove the cattle to the edge of a ravine and held them there the entire afternoon while the rain continued to fall. When the weather cleared up, the men went out to retrieve the animals that had gotten away. Burgos saw a calf that was drowning in a lagoon that had formed in a hollow. It must have had a broken leg, because every time it tried to climb out, it slid back in. He lassoed it from above and held it up by its neck. The animal twisted around and kicked the air in desperation. It got away from him and fell back into the water. The calf's head floated in the lagoon. Burgos lassoed it again. The calf was kicking its legs and gasping for air. The other men gathered around the edge of the deep hollow. This time Burgos held it up for a while, and then let it drop. The calf sank and took a while to resurface.

The men started making comments to each other. Burgos lassoed it and raised it up, and when the calf was near the top, he dropped it again. The men reacted with shouts and loud laughter. Burgos repeated the operation several times. The animal would try to avoid the lasso and would sink back into the water. When it tried to swim away, the men urged Burgos to fish it out again. The game went on for a while, amid jokes and jests, until Burgos finally lassoed the calf out, after it had nearly drowned, and lifted it up slowly to the feet of his horse. The animal was lying in the mud, gasping for air, its eyes white with fright. Then one of the men jumped off his horse and cut its throat with one quick slash.

"It's done, kid," he said to Burgos; "tonight we're having barbecued fish for dinner." Everyone broke out in loud laughter, and for the first time in a long time Burgos felt the respect and the comradeship of the men.

Macedonio was always gathering strange stories. Even when he was a treasurer in the Province of Misiones, he was already compiling anecdotes and stories. "Stories have simple hearts, just like women. Or men. But I prefer to say women," Macedonio would say, "because it makes me think of Scheherazade." It was not until much later, Junior thought, that they understood what he was trying to say. Around that time Macedonio had lost his wife, Elena Obieta, and everything that Macedonio did since then (and especially the machine) was meant to make her seem present. She was the Eternal One, the river of stories, the endless voice that kept memory alive. He never accepted the fact that he had lost her. In this he was like Dante. And, like Dante, he built a world in which he could live with her. The machine was that world, it was his masterpiece. He got her out of nowhere and kept her covered with a blanket on the floor of a closet in the room of a boardinghouse around Tribunales, near the courthouse. The system was simple, he had hit on it by accident. When it transformed "William Wilson" into the story of Stephen Stevensen, Macedonio realized that he had the basic elements from which he could build a virtual reality. So he began working with series and variables. First he thought about the English railroads and the reading of novels. The genre grew in the nineteenth century, it was tied in with the mode of transportation. That is why so many stories take place on trains. People liked to read stories about a train while they rode aboard a train. In Argentina, the first train ride in a novel is clearly found in the work of Cambaceres.

In one of the rooms of the Museum Junior saw the train car in which Erdosain had killed himself. It was dark green, bloodstains could be seen on one of the leather seats, the windows were open. In the other room he saw the photograph of a train car that belonged to the old Ferrocarril Central Argentino. That was the car in which the woman who fled at dawn traveled. Junior imagined her nodding off in her seat, the train cutting through the darkness of the country, all its windows lit up. That was one of the first stories.

A WOMAN

She had a two-year-old son but decided to abandon him. She tied him with a long belt to a hoop on the ceiling and left him crawling around in the room on a waterproof rug. She took the precaution of moving the furniture and piling it up against the walls, far from the child's reach, so it would be like an empty room. She wrote a note to the cleaning woman, telling her she had gone out to run an errand. It was seven in the morning. The moment her husband drove off to work in his car, she called a taxi and took the first long-distance train out of Retiro Station. The next day she was in a small town on the border of the Province of San Luis. In the hotel she signed in under her mother's name (Lía Matra). She spent the day sleeping and at night went down to gamble in the casino. The roulette was like the face of fortune. The men and women in the hall went there looking for answers, each in an isolated microscopic universe. (Those funereal croupiers, she thought, she would have liked to take one of them to bed with her.) It was a poor casino, with light-blue carpeting. She imagined that Hell must have the same decor. A half empty and poorly lit room, with an "electric" blue moquette. The men wore jackets, the women looked like retired bar girls. A cloud of insects buzzing around an artificial replica of passion and life. The woman thought of days or months and played them in progression and always won. When the casino closed they gave her the money she had won in a paper bag. She had to cross a plaza in order to get back to the hotel. There was a statue, benches, a garbage can chained to a tree. She was going to call home and let them know she had left. The woman hides the bag with the money in the bushes. The town is empty, a light shines in the distance where the old train station used to be. The woman crosses the street, goes up to her room, and only then decides to unpack her suitcase. She hangs her clothes up in the closet, arranges her bottles and creams in the cabinet in the restroom, closes the windows so the daylight will not come in. Calls down to the front desk, asks not to be disturbed, then kills herself.

The room in which the woman committed suicide was reproduced in the Museum. Junior saw the picture of the son against the lamp on the night table. He did not remember this detail from the story. The series of hotel rooms was reproduced in successive halls. The boardinghouse in which an old man sat on a wicker chair and plucked at a guitar through the night. The washbasin on the iron base in which a German soldier's lover had washed her hair. Junior saw the hotel room from Cuernavaca, the bed surrounded by a mosquito netting and a bottle of tequila. In another hall to the side was the room from the Majestic and the armoire in which the woman had looked for the bottle of perfume. He was astonished by the precision of the reconstruction. It seemed like a dream. But dreams were false stories. And these were true stories. Each one isolated in a corner of the Museum, building the story of their lives. Everything was as it should be. Military uniforms in tall glass cases, Moreira's long dagger on a black velvet pillow, the photograph of a laboratory in one of the islands of the Tigre Delta. The stories were developed from these objects. They were crisp and clear as memories. The last room contained the mirror, and in the mirror was the first love story.

FIRST LOVE

I fell in love for the first time when I was twelve years old. A redhead showed up in the middle of the school year. The teacher introduced her as the new student. She was standing next to the blackboard, her name was (or is) Clara Schultz. I do not remember anything from the weeks that followed, but I do know that we fell in love, and that we tried to hide it because we knew we were too young and that what we wanted was impossible. Some of the memories still hurt now. The others would look at us when we stood in line together, and she would turn even redder, and I learned what it meant to suffer the complicity of those fools. I got into fights after school in the small soccer field on Amenedo with guys from the fifth and sixth grades who used to follow her around and throw thistles in her hair—just because she wore it loose and it came down to her waist. One afternoon, I came home so beat up that my mother thought that I must have been crazy, or that I had contracted some kind of suicidal fever. I could not tell anyone what I was feeling. I looked surly and sullen, as if I were always tired. We wrote each other letters, although we barely knew how to write. I remember living through an unstable succession of feelings that alternated between ecstasy and desperation. I remember that she was serious and passionate and that she never smiled, perhaps because she knew what the future held in store for us. I do not have any photographs of her, only my memories, but Clara has been present in every woman I have ever loved. She left just as she had arrived, unexpectedly, before the end of the year. One afternoon she did something heroic. Breaking all the rules, she came running into the boys patio, which was forbidden to girls, to tell me that they were taking her away. I can still see the two of us standing on the red bricks of the patio, the others in a circle around us, looking on sarcastically. Her father was a municipal inspector or a manager in a bank and was being transferred to Sierra de la Ventana. I remember the horror that the image of a sierra that was also a jail produced in me. That is why she had arrived in the middle of the school year, and perhaps also why she had loved me. My pain was more than I could stand, but I managed to remember that my mother used to say that if you loved someone you should put a mirror under your pillow, and that if you saw that person reflected in your dreams, it meant you would get married. At night, when everyone at home had gone to sleep, I would walk barefoot to the back patio and take the mirror in which my father shaved every morning off the hook. It was a square mirror, with a brown wooden frame, and a small chain in the back from where it hung on a nail in the wall. I would sleep and wake up frequently at night, trying to see her reflection when I dreamt. At times I imagined that I saw her beginning to appear in the corner of the mirror. One night, many years later, I dreamt that I was dreaming with her in the mirror. I saw her just as she was when she was a girl, with her red hair and her serious eyes. I was completely different, but she was the same, and she was walking toward me, as if she were my daughter.

The mirror's wooden frame was marked with gray notches, as if someone had chiseled it with a letter opener. Junior looked at his own face and saw the gallery reflected behind him. The guard had been following him silently at a distance. But now he walked up to him, one hand behind his back and the specter of the other in his pocket, and swallowed, or so Junior thought from the movement of his Adam's apple.

"What's that?" Junior asked, pointing to a glass box.

"Science has not yet been able to determine its nature," he answered with an obviously memorized phrase. "A vulture, or perhaps a chimango. It was found in 1895 in the area outside Tapalqué by Doctor Roger Fontaine, a French scientist," he said as his shaking finger pointed at the bronze placard.

Inside the case there was a metal bird perched on a branch, pecking at one of its wings.

"Strange," Junior said.

"And now look at this skull," the guard said. "It's from the same region."

It looked like a glass cranium. The Argentine countryside is inexhaustible. In small towns people hold onto the remnants of the oldest of stories.

Next to it there was a series of objects lined up inside a low glass cabinet, all made out of bone. They looked like dice, or small knucklebones with which boys might play, or heretical rosary beads. Junior stopped to look at a Japanese vase, probably donated by some navy officer. He had seen a replica at the market in Plaza Francia, they could make reproductions so precise that they were better than the original. They could even get the copy to look older and more pure. The guard had disappeared quietly out a side stairwell. Junior walked through a gallery containing drawings and photographs from the police archives, and entered another hall. It was a room in a family's house, the blinds drawn and a lamplight on, without any furniture. A little further down, almost at floor level, in the middle of the room, as if it were in a cradle, was the doll.

The Girl

The matrimony's first two children were able to lead a normal life, especially considering the difficulties associated with having a sister like her in a small town. The girl (Laura) was born healthy. It was only with time that they began to notice certain strange signs. Her system of hallucinations was the topic of a complicated report that appeared in a scientific journal, but her father had deciphered it long before that. Yves Fonagy called it "extravagant references." In these highly unusual cases the patient imagines that everything that occurs around him is a projection of his personality. The patient excludes real people from his experience, because he considers himself much more intelligent than anyone else. The world was an extension of herself; her body spread outward and reproduced itself. She was constantly preoccupied by mechanical objects, especially electric lightbulbs. She saw them as words, every time one was turned on it was like someone had begun to speak. Thus she considered darkness to be a form of silent thinking. One summer afternoon (when she was five years old) she looked at an electric fan spinning on a dresser. She thought it was a living being, a female living being. The girl of the air, her soul trapped in a cage. Laura said that she lived "there," and raised her hand to indicate the ceiling. There, she said, moving her head from left to right. Her mother turned off the fan. That is when she began having difficulties with language. She lost the capacity to use personal pronouns. With time she stopped using them altogether, then hid all the words she knew in her memory. She would only utter a little clucking sound as she opened and closed her eyes. The mother separated the boys from their sister because she was afraid that it was contagious. One of those small town beliefs. But madness is not contagious and the girl was not crazy. In any case, they sent the two brothers to a Catholic boarding school in Del Valle, and the family went into seclusion in their large house in Bolívar. The father was a frustrated musician who taught mathematics in the public high school. The mother was a teacher and had become principal, but she decided to retire in order to take care of her daughter. They did not want to have her committed. So they took her twice a week to an institute in La Plata and followed the orders given by Doctor Arana, who treated her with electric shock therapy. He explained that the girl lived in an extreme emotional void. That is why Laura's language was slowly becoming more and more abstract and unpersonalized. At first she still used the correct names for food. She would say "butter," "sugar," "water," but later began to refer to different food items in groups that were disconnected from their nutritive nature. Sugar became "white sand," butter, "soft mud," water, "wet air." It was clear that by disarranging the names and abandoning personal pronouns she was creating a language that better corresponded to her personal emotional experiences. Far from not knowing how to use words correctly, what could be seen was a spontaneous decision to create a language that matched her experience of the world. Doctor Arana did not agree, but this was the father's hypothesis, and he decided to enter his daughter's verbal world. She was a logic machine connected to the incorrect interface. The girl functioned according to the model of a fan—a fixed rotational axis served as her syntactic schema, and she moved her head as she spoke to feel the wind of her unarticulated thoughts. The decision to teach her how to use language implied also having to explain to her how to compartmentalize words. But she would lose them like molecules in warm air. Her memory was a breeze blowing in the white curtains of a room in an empty house. It was necessary to try to take that sailboat out in still air. The father stopped going to Doctor Arana's clinic and began treating the girl with a singing teacher. He had to give her a temporal sequence, and he believed that music was an abstract model of the order of things in the world. She sang Mozart arias in German with Madame Silenzky, a Polish pianist who directed the chorus in the Lutheran Church in Carhué. The girl, sitting on the bench, howled to the rhythm. Madame Silenzky was frightened to death because she thought the child was a monster. She was twelve years old, fat and beautiful like a madonna, but her eyes looked as if they were made out of glass and she clucked before singing. Madame Silenzky thought the girl was a hybrid, a doll made out of foam, a human machine, without feelings, without hope. She screamed more than she sang, always out of tune, but eventually she was able to follow the line of a melody. Her father was trying to get her to incorporate a temporal memory, an empty form, composed of rhythmic sequences and modulations. The girl did not have any syntax (she lacked the very notion of syntax). She lived in a wet universe, time for her was a hand-washed sheet that you wring out in the middle to get the water out. She has staked out her own territory, her father would say, from which she wishes to exclude all experiences. Anything new, any event that she has not yet experienced and which is still to be lived, seems like something painful, like something threatening and terrifying to her. The petrified present, the monstrous and viscous and solid stoppage of time, the chronological void, can only be altered with music. Music is not an experience, it is the pure form of life, it has no content, it cannot frighten her, her father would say, and Madame Silenzky (terrified) would shake her gray head and relax her hands on the piano keys by playing a Haydn cantata before they began. When he finally got the girl to enter a temporal sequence, the mother fell ill and had to be hospitalized. The girl associated her mother's disappearance (she died two months later) with a Schubert lied. She sang the melody as if she were crying over someone's death and remembering a lost past. Then, using his daughter's musical syntax as a base, the father began working on her lexicon. The girl did not have any form from which to construct references, it was like teaching a foreign language to a dead person. (Like teaching a dead language to a foreigner.) He decided to begin by telling her short stories. The girl stood still, near the light, in the hall facing the patio. The father would sit in an armchair and narrate a story to her as if he were singing. He hoped the sentences would enter his daughter's memory like blocks of meaning. That is why he chose to tell her the same story, only varying the version each time. The plot would become the sole model of the world and the sentences modulations of possible experiences. The story was a simple one. In his *Chronicle of the Kings of England* (twelfth century), William of Malmesbury tells the story of a young, sovereign Roman noble who has just gotten married. After the feasts and the celebrations, the young man and his friends go out to play bocci balls in the garden. In the course of the game, the young man puts his wedding ring, to avoid losing it, on the barely extended finger of the hand of a bronze statue. When he goes to retrieve it, he finds that the statue's hand is now a tight fist, and he cannot get his ring back. Without telling anyone, he comes back at night with torches and servants and discovers that the statue has disappeared. He keeps the truth from his bride, but when he gets into bed that night, he feels that there is something between them, something dense and hazy that prevents them from embracing. Terrified, he hears a voice that murmurs in his ear:

"Kiss me, today you and I were united in matrimony. I am Venus, and you have given me the ring of love."

The first time he told the story, the girl seemed to fall asleep. There was a breeze from the garden at the end of the patio. There were no visible changes, at night she dragged herself into her room and curled up in the darkness with her normal clucking. The next day, at the same time, her father sat her in the same place and told her another version of the story. The first important variation had appeared about twenty years later, in a German compilation from the mid–twelfth century titled *Kaiserchronik*. In this version, the statue on whose finger the young man places the ring is not Venus, but the Virgin Mary. When he tries to unite with his bride, the Mother of God comes between the couple to chastise him, which incites a mystical passion in the young man. After leaving his wife, the young man becomes a priest and devotes the rest of his life to the service of Our Lady. An anonymous twelfth-century painting depicts the Virgin Mary with a ring on her left ring finger and an enigmatic smile on her lips.

Every day, in the early evening, the father would tell her the same story in its multiple variations. The clucking girl was an anti-Scheherazade, she heard the story of the ring told a thousand and one times at night by her father. Within a year the girl is already smiling, because she knows how the story ends. Sometimes she looks down at her hands and moves her fingers, as if she were the statue. She looks up at the garden and, for the first time, gives her version of the events in a soft whisper. "Mouvo looked at the night. Where his face had been another appeared, Kenya's. Again the strange laugh. All of a sudden Mouvo was in a corner of the house and Kenya in the garden and the sensorial circles of the ring were very sad," she said. From that point on, with the repertory of words she had learned and with the circular structure of the story, she began to build a language, an uninterrupted series of phrases that allowed her to communicate with her father. In the following months she was the one who told the story, every evening, in the hall facing the patio in the back of the house. She reached a point where she was able to tell, word for word, the version by Henry James—perhaps because his story, "The Last of the Valerii," was the last in the series. (The action has shifted to Rome in the time of the Risorgimento, where a young woman, who has inherited a fortune, in one of those typically Jamesian moves, marries an Italian noble from a distinguished, but impoverished, lineage. One afternoon, a group of laborers working at a dig in the gardens of the villa discover a statue of Juno. *Signor Conte* begins to feel a strange fascination with that masterpiece from the best period of Greek sculpture. He moves the statue to an abandoned greenhouse and hides it mistrustfully from anyone's view. In the days that follow, he transfers a large part of the passion he feels for his beautiful wife to the marble statue, and spends more and more of his time in the glass structure. At the end, the *Contessa,* in order to free her husband from the spell, tears the ring off of the goddess's ring finger and buries it at the far end of the gardens. Her life becomes happy once again.) A gentle drizzle was falling in the patio and the father was rocking in his chair. That afternoon the girl left the story for the first time, she left the closed circle of the story like someone walking through a door, and asked her father to buy her a gold ring (*anello*). There she was, singing softly, clucking, a sad music machine. She was sixteen years old, a pale dreamer, like a Greek statue. As steadfast as an angel.

Junior saw the ring and the succession of the different versions of the story of the ring. An engraving by Dürer ("Melancholy," 1497–98) hung on the wall to the left. Passion, symbolized by the figure of Venus, with a ring in her left hand and a stone sphere at her feet. The story was the tale of the power of stories, the song of the girl looking for life, the music of words repeated to form a closed circle of gold. Off to a side there was a copy of *The Anatomy of Melancholy,* with notes and drawings written inside. Burton had also told the story of the ring in order to illustrate the power of love. The girl lives again thanks to her father's stories. To narrate was to give life to a statue, to give life to someone who was afraid of living. One of the glass cabinets contained an original copy of the first myth. "He who has lost his wife works relentlessly to build a statue, thinking about her all the time. To live alone or to build the lost woman for oneself. Passion allows the man in love to opt for the latter dream. The *Gesta Romanorum* (the most popular storybook of the Middle Ages) tells us that Virgil, who considered himself a magician (Story LVII), used to sculpt magic statues to preserve the souls of his dead friends. The ability to give life to an inanimate object is a faculty associated with the idea of the thaumaturge and the powers of a sorcerer. In Egyptian, the word 'sculptor' literally means 'he who keeps life.' In the ancient burial rites it was believed that the soul of the deceased traveled to a statue of his body, and a ceremony was held to celebrate the transition from body to statue." Junior recalled the photograph of Elena, the young woman with the turtleneck sweater and the plaid skirt, smiling at the invisible light. A photograph was also a mirror in which to dream a lost woman. There was an enlarged reproduction of the same picture of Elena on the wall at the far end of the room. He saw Macedonio's manuscripts behind several glass panels. "To escape toward the indefinite spaces of future forms. The possible is what spreads forth into existence. That which can be imagined occurs and goes on to become a part of reality." Macedonio was not trying to build a replica of man, but rather a machine that could produce replicas. His goal was to nullify death and construct a virtual world. "The country-city, with a million small farms and ten thousand factories," Junior read, "completely exempt from the horror of the word 'rent,' would have the advantages presented in the following list: Military unattackability. Unattackability via siege or blockade. No firemen. No policemen. A despairing scarcity of diseases. A reduction of more than 40 percent of all speculative, unproductive, barren and aleatory commercial exchanges." Junior looked at the end of the letter. "The war is coming to an end. All that will be left for us is the dark overbearing plans of the United States, which wants to strike Spain and seize power from her to more easily capture Spanish America. The islands have been occupied, the lab must be saved. Very truly yours, Macedonio." He looked at the signature, at that frail and immortal handwriting, and then walked around the hall, keeping his distance from the machine. It was smooth and slender and seemed to have a pulsing intermittent light. It is only reading me, Junior thought. There are others, in other isolated galleries, reliving their own memories. There was no one else in the room. He thought he saw a flashlight shining on the tiles of the floor, coming toward him from the end of the hallway. As if someone had gotten off a train in a lost station in the middle of the night, Junior thought, and was now slicing through a field, the flashlight shining on the grass. Far off, in what seemed to be the haze of dawn, the Korean appeared, walking in a dream. He was climbing down the ramp that led to the basement and the lower rooms of the Museum with difficulty, dragging his left leg. He looked like a jockey with frightened eyes. It's Fuyita, Junior thought. He was wearing a black tie and a strip of black silk on the sleeve of his coat indicating he was in mourning. Junior thought of the woman locked in the room of the Majestic Hotel. The men barely acknowledged each other, then Fuyita walked down the corridor and Junior followed him.

"I have some material that I would like you to analyze, Mr. Junior. The newspaper must hold off, though, until we let you know that it is okay to publish the information. You get my drift?" he asked Junior once they had sat at a table in the café on the first floor, near the window facing the greenhouses. "Don't pay any attention to what those women may have said about me. Madness takes over the heart and the truth gets lost. I'm a spy, a foreigner, I'd like to return to my native home. Now, I want you to know that I'm working for Richter, the Engineer. It is imperative that you talk to him, he is perfectly aware of the situation. He has collaborated with Macedonio from the beginning, he has the proofs and the documents. They want to nullify us, but we will resist. We," the jockey said to Junior, "led by the Engineer, have many drafts and multiple stories. We have gotten a hold of an absolutely secret text, for example, one of the machine's last stories, or perhaps the last, because there was a series of six unpublished stories, and one that was released, and then a series of three, and finally two more, published before she was declared out of commission."

He spoke in a frozen whisper, his small catfish-eyes fixed on Junior's face. He began to tell him the story of Richter, the Engineer, a German physicist who came to get away from the Nazis at the start of the war, and worked on the plans and the programming of the machine, and then became a businessman, and mounted an agricultural-industrial complex in a small town in the province of Buenos Aires that went bankrupt. "After Macedonio's death, the Engineer withdrew to his abandoned, bankrupt factory. The installations were all held up. He prepared to wage another battle while his mother roamed around in the upper floors, because by this time," the jockey told him, "the Engineer spoke only to his mother, who is crazy but he does not want to have her hospitalized—dedicated as he is to planning an Institute of Agro-Industrial Development and to not think about the machine. Because the Engineer always tried to keep his family problems—in other words, his mother—separate from problems that arose from his dreams—in other words, the machine." This guy is crazy, Junior thought, he is trying to confuse me.

"How much money do you need?" Junior asked, suddenly cutting him off.

Fuyita smiled at him with his thin mustache and his fish-face, and started talking with a Korean accent.

"No, don't need money, no, no money, your paper want information, yes, we give you facts, because we don't want machine disactivated," he said. "Understand?"

"Yes," Junior said. "Okay."

"Maybe you want I tell you how the Engineer he meet Macedonio, and how they start working together, but there is plenty time and anyway you must go to island and visit him in his factory and speak to him. Look," he said, and showed him the documents. He placed special emphasis on a folder that contained the story that he had had delivered to the Engineer, and that the jockey had had photocopied to give to Junior with the idea, if it was at all possible, of making the first move in a counteroffensive.

"Political power is always criminal," Fuyita said. "The president is crazy and his ministers are all psychopaths. The Argentine State is telepathic, its intelligence services can read minds from a distance. It can infiltrate the thoughts of the bases. But telepathic faculties have a serious drawback. They are unable to select and filter, they receive all kinds of information, they are too sensitive to people's marginal thoughts, to what the old-school psychologists used to call the unconscious. Faced with an excess of facts, they expand the radius of repression. The machine has been able to infiltrate their networks, they are no longer able to distinguish between true stories and false versions. There is a certain relationship between telepathic faculties and television," he said all of a sudden, "the technical-myopic lens of the camera records and transmits the repressed, hostile thoughts of the masses and converts them into images. To watch TV is to read the thoughts of a million people. Are you following me here?"

He was a gangster and a philosopher. Oriental traditions, Junior thought, martial arts and Zen Buddhism. He is in mourning over the emperor's death and leaves the girl locked up in the hotel as if she were a cat. On the other side of the glass, in the greenhouse, a man was strolling through the flowers with a lantern in his hand.

"Have you seen the blue roses?" the jockey asked. "They make them in Temperley, there are three in the Museum, they are very difficult to preserve. You have to use liquid ice and silver nitrate. First came the bronze rose, but you cannot get them anymore, that site has been closed down several times by the police. They use a different excuse every time. If it were up to them, they would show up with a new search warrant each time just to stroll through the nurseries with the carnivorous plants and the poppy plants."

They went down together in the pneumatic elevator, the jockey balancing on his right leg. In this manner he avoided setting his left one down, which he had injured in a straight-line race in Isidro Casanove. He had been riding a horse named Small Wolf, with a white spot on its forehead, in a historic meet with the undefeated horse of the widow of an Englishman who had been the director of the Argentine Central Railroad before it was nationalized. He had driven the horse as hard as he could, because the widow bet like a gypsy, and as soon as they started Small Wolf began to pant in a bloody whine, but he kept him going straight and stayed in the lead for nearly a mile, until the horse collapsed, its heart failed, and it rolled over its rider. Fuyita's left leg was crushed by the horse's body and there was no way to repair the tiny broken bones in his ankle.

"I don't use a walking stick," the jockey said affectedly as he crossed the circular room where the machine was displayed, "because I believe that medicine will be able to cure me, and I don't want to get used to being an invalid." Junior thought the jockey had a smooth gracefulness that was accentuated by his limp. When they stopped at the ramp that led to the exit he tried to clear his mind and not think of anything.

"A woman sent me to see you," he said then.

"She calls you, too?" Fuyita asked. "At night? And talks to you about her son?"

"Her husband," Junior said.

"It's the same thing," Fuyita said.

"You know her?" Junior asked, showing him the photograph of the young woman.

"That's Elena," Fuyita said. "She was the girl of his dreams. These women," he said, "we follow them around and chase after them as if we were dumbstruck cops." He turned toward the Museum entrance. All the lights were on, people were waiting in line to get in. "Take this," he said, "be careful." He handed him a manila envelope, then smiled and flagged a taxi. Junior got into the car, but after he had settled in he thought Fuyita had wanted to say something else to him, because he saw him gesturing with his arms and his lips moving. He stuck his head out the window, but the jockey waved him off because the roar of the city drowned out his voice. Besides, the cab took off down the avenue just then, and disappeared along the park heading west.

Junior laid down in the backseat. The Museum clock read three P.M. He opened the envelope. The story was called "The White Nodes." An explosive story, the paranoid ramifications of life in the city. That's why there's so much control, Junior thought, they're trying to erase what's recorded in the streets. A light bright as a flash on the ashen faces of innocent people in the photographs of police dossiers.

The White Nodes

She knew the Clinic was a sinister place. When Doctor Arana came in, he confirmed her worst fears. He seemed to be there just to make every single paranoid delirium come true. A glass skull, the red windows facing out, white bones shining in the artificial light. Elena thought the man was a magnet that attracted and drew the iron shavings of the soul to itself. She was already thinking like a madwoman. She felt her skin release a metal dust. That is why her body was completely covered, including gloves and a long-sleeved blouse. The only part exposed was her face, the rusted skin of her external gears. It made her sick to think about the metal container from which they would put the drops of oil on her. She closed her eyes so she would not see anything, and began to go over what she knew about the doctor. *Arana, Raúl, Ph.D. in Psychiatry. Disciple of Carl Jung. Studies undertaken in Germany and Switzerland.* The treatment consisted in converting psychotics into addicts. The drugs were administered every three hours. The only way to normalize a delirium was to create an extreme dependency. He had just returned from giving a seminar at MIT on "Hypochondria and the Fantasies of Pregnancy." Elena had herself committed with the double purpose of carrying out an investigation and of controlling her hallucinations. She was sure that she had died and that someone had transferred her brain (sometimes she said her soul) into a machine. She felt she was completely alone in a white room full of tubes and cables. It was not a nightmare, it was the certainty that the man who loved her had saved her from death and had incorporated her into an apparatus that transmitted her thoughts. She was eternal and cursed. (You cannot have one without the other.) That is why the judge had chosen her to infiltrate the Clinic. A male nurse met her at the entrance. As soon as she walked through the bars she decided she would tell them the truth. She was a madwoman who believed she was a policewoman who was forced to be hospitalized in a psychiatric clinic; and she was a policewoman trained to pretend that she was in a machine exhibited in a room of a Museum. (The only thing she had to do was not reveal the name of a certain man, whom she would call Mac from now on. Anything else, including the truth, would be an invention in which to hide and keep him safe.)

"That is why you say that you never lie," Doctor Arana said, smiling.

"I did not say that," Elena said, "do not play dumb. I have been asked to investigate you, doctor, that is why I am here."

He turned around and smiled again.

"Very well," he said, "come with me."

The hallway led to the operating rooms. The rubber carpets prevented all electrical contact and negated the friction from the aluminum wheels. The trees in the garden could be seen through the tall windows.

"And who gave you this assignment?"

"A judge," she answered.

There were bars in front of the windows, and a portrait of Doctor Arana on the wall. Many of his patients were painters who paid him with their own work.

"They are going to flatten this pigsty."

"What does it mean to be a machine?" Doctor Arana asked.

"Nothing," she said. "A machine does not exist, a machine functions."

"Very ingenious," Arana replied.

The Clinic was a large rectangular construction, divided into zones and pavilions, like a jail.

"In this first room you have the catatonics. They are completely gone," Arana explained; "technically, they have gone over to the other side and cannot return."

The beds looked as if they held embalmed bodies, a series of white mummies wrapped in sheets and blankets. A woman sitting in a metal chair was staring at the light in the window. Elena tried to take note of the layout of the alarms and the side doors. She was going to escape as soon as she managed to see Mac, she thought they had him locked up in one of the wings by the end of the garden. She had drawn up a map in her memory and was completing the diagram as they went along. She worked with a scale of 100 to 2, to make the information easier to transmit. Each zone had its own control unit and surveillance system. The small cameras were mounted on the ceilings. Elena imagined the closed-circuit and the control room. She had once seen the intelligence center for Penn Station in New York. All the passengers were recorded in the hallways and the platforms, and a policewoman (a real policewoman)—fat, with makeup, black glasses, and dressed in blue—sat on a rotating chair, alone in a white basement, surrounded by TV screens, watching the images that covered the walls. She had a microphone attached to her blouse that captured her voice and her breathing. In the bathrooms, men addicted to vices pursued those vices. She spied on them and relayed the information to the patrols working on the surface. Three policemen were kicking a junkie on the floor of the hallway that led to platform number six (the exit toward Jamaica Station, in Long Island). They were in the section of the Clinic that contained the *Carson Café*. A bar that looked as if it were from the fifties, with dim lights and tables against the walls. A place where expatriates, spies, foreign journalists, and married women looking to hook up spent their time.

"They call it the Bar of the Lost Souls," Arana explained.

Elena found a place at the bar. She wanted a beer. The bartender smiled. Perhaps they had already given her the injection. Imaginary landscapes had been fully explored by Doctor Arana. Reality was made up of personal visions. The Clinic was the inner city and each person saw what they wanted to. No one seemed to have their own personal memories. The bartender treated her as if she were a friend of his. In the mirror, Elena saw her mother's face in her house in Olavarría. Everyone was an addict, submerged in their own deliriums and ghettos, using their own personal hermetic metaphors. The guy next to her at the bar introduced himself by raising his glass.

"My name is Luca Lombardo," he said. "I'm from Rosario, they call me the Tano, they locked me up here for my own protection. What took place in the province of Santa Fe is a tragedy, they killed children, women, the men had to show the palms of their hands and if they saw that they were laborers they'd shoot them right there on the spot. The only thing left is the desert and the river. Many escaped to the islands and are living in the middle of the tall bamboo plants. They live like Indians, in the Lechiguanas Islands, wherever they can, they heat water in little pans to make *mate*. They're waiting for the soldiers to leave."

The Tano stared at the bottles behind the counter as he spoke. The bar was packed. A disc jockey put on an album by The Hunger. Mobs of people were roaming through the place. They all looked alike, sallow and dressed in fringed shirts and leather. Lumpen from the surrounding hotels and tense solitary tourists in search of pleasures not indicated in Michelin Guides. Very old or very young men walked in discontinuous waves in opposite directions. The attractive women, on the other hand, with their prostheses and their melancholy eyes, stood to the side, in the corners, or sat at the bar, like Elena. At that time of day the halls with the games of logic were already open. In the place across the way Elena saw a very young super-D with eight-diopter glasses solving syllogisms at supersonic speeds. He caught them in the air and ran up points with the elegance of a bird. His opponent was a shy and smiling youth with a dark complexion who spoke with a sing-songy Paraguayan accent and was the best Frege semanticist in the city. He read a comic book calmly as he waited his turn, sneaking glances out the side of his magazine at the rising scores of the super-D youngster.

"So you are willing to collaborate with us," Doctor Arana asked her.

"In exchange for what?" Elena asked.

She was trying to buy time and put together a line of defense. She was afraid of betraying herself and being forced to inform. She knew about the ones who went out into the streets and sold out everyone they knew. They wore masks made of synthetic skins and rode for hours in patrol cars through the center of the city.

"In exchange for curing you," Arana said.

"I am not interested in being cured, I just want to change hallucinations. Is that possible?"

Arana served himself some mineral water in a plastic cup.

"We could disconnect you," he said, "but that is very expensive."

"Money is not an issue with me," she said.

"It will be necessary to work on your memory," Arana said. "There are areas of condensation, white nodes, which can be untied, opened up. They are like myths," he said; "they define the grammar of experience. Everything the linguists have taught us about language also applies to the core of living matter. The genetic code and the verbal code present us with the same characteristics. That is what we call the white nodes. The clinic neurologists can attempt an intervention. It will be necessary to work on your brain."

They were going to operate on her. She felt sluggish and empty, she was afraid they had disconnected her.

She thought about the Tano, running away from Rosario, saying he belonged to the PRA, the People's Revolutionary Army, but the PRA no longer existed. She pictured him going in and out of detox clinics, lost in a virtual reality, hidden in clandestine houses and getting caught again, evading the controls, living in subways. He was a rebel and she was the heroine, a Mata Hari, a double agent, a confidant for anyone in dire straits. She had to get out, return to the streets. She saw the Tano's room in the Bajo, near the port. She was going to contact him, he was the only one who could plan an escape for her. But she had to forget, she could not compromise the plans. She destroyed the meeting on the platform at Retiro Station, the bums toasting stale bread over a small fire, the Tano and her getting on the train. She knew how to erase her thoughts, like someone forgetting a word they were about to say. They would not be able to make her talk about what she did not know. A navy officer appeared, and she thought she saw armed men in the hallway behind him.

"See, captain," Arana said, "this woman says that she is a machine."

"Very beautiful," said the man dressed in white.

Elena looked at him with scorn and hatred.

"You're an ex, there are only patients here."

Arana smiled as the light slid down his skin. He had aluminum teeth, a very expensive ultralight crown of the kind only made by Gucci, the artist, in the clinics in Belgrano R neighborhood.

"Take it easy," he said. "If you want to be cured, you have to collaborate with us. The captain will help you remember. He is a specialist in artificial memory."

"Madam," the officer said, "we would like to know who Mac is."

They knew everything. She had to escape. She had fallen asleep, but now she was awake and made an effort to keep going. It was getting dark, the light from the large billboards was starting to fill the air with bright faces and images. The Tano came out of the subway and up an escalator at Diagonal Station. The pleasant spring breeze and the smell of the lime trees in the avenue produced a sudden happiness in her. Elena leaned against the window of the Trust Jeweler shop. Multiple clocks read 3 P.M. They had merged the time zones everywhere in the world so they could coordinate the eight o'clock news. They had to live at night while the sun rose in Tokyo. It was better this way, the endless darkness worked to their benefit, they had nearly fifteen hours to get across the city and out to the open country. She pictured the still Pampas, the last towns like hills in the distance. They had already decided they would go live with the Irish, the Tano knew how to get into the Delta and meet up with the rebel ghettos. She had heard about Finnegans Isle, far up the Paraná River, on the other side of the Liffey, perhaps they could make it that far. It was populated by anarchists, the children and grandchildren of British settlers from Santa Cruz and Chubut Provinces. The Tano walked toward her among the crowd of workers and policemen and Bolivian immigrants heading south on Cerrito, downtown. She could make out his set, massive figure in the sea of anonymous faces. All of them, and perhaps she as well, in a hospital bed.

"Then," Arana said, "where did you meet him?"

"In a boardinghouse in Tribunales, near the courthouse," she said.

She was afraid. They were getting closer to the truth, as if they could follow the road of the memories of her life on a map. They seemed to know more about her than she did. She was lying on an iron bed, she had the sensation of being opened up and felt the freezing air from the fan on her bones. The amphetamines were making her hallucinate, her thoughts were racing much faster than she could articulate them, ideas transformed into real images. She could not stop, she would awake from one dream and into another reality, she would find herself in a different room, in another life, she did not want to fall asleep again. If she could only live in an eternal state of insomnia. He never slept. He would rest, but he did not sleep, he watched over her while she was in the hospital, not daring to enter her room, he looked in from the outside, through the windows that faced the patio. He stayed awake through the nights, sitting on the cretonne couches in the waiting room. He was afraid that the doctors would inject her with anesthesia and take her to the operating rooms. Then they would be able to process her memory and unrecord the information. As long as she was in the machine, she could overcome matter and resist. "A body," Mac said, "does not mean anything, the soul is the only thing that is alive, and it takes the shape of the word." She knew that the anarchs had infiltrated several men into the Clinic. They had given her the name of a contact to use in case of a desperate situation. Reyes. A woman in the Majestic. For the time being she did not want to think about him. But it seemed to her that everywhere around her there were letters forming the word "Reyes." Mr. Reyes, a dealer and a gangster and a professor of English literature. The crowd was getting thicker, making it more and more difficult for her to move forward. The Tano stood there, pale, taciturn, more melancholy than usual. He had run out of money, had spent the last of what he had on a taxi. He was the best explosives technician that they had ever had, and he did not want to have any problems with the police. Elena went up to him when they stopped at a red light. The cars headed down Av. Corrientes in discontinuous waves.

"We have to get to the island," she said without looking at him. "I have a contact, but I am being watched."

"Everyone is being watched," he answered. And smiled at her. When he smiled he looked like a madman. Then he glanced at her out of the corner of his eye. "The first thing is to get into the Museum," he said to her. "There's nothing there anymore, it's been abandoned, there are only a few remnants left."

They were in the Carabelas alleyway, behind the enormous concrete building that housed the Mercado del Plata. The site had been used as barracks during the war, and old faded photographs of Perón still covered the walls. A multitude of refugees and vagrants proliferated through the galleries. The police did not dare enter the building, but the place was infected with government agents. She had the feeling of being lost, of having lost her sense of reality.

"You have lost your sense of reality," Arana said to her, as if he were reading her mind. Maybe she was thinking out loud.

"This is a place without memories," she said. "Everyone pretends to be somebody else. The spies are trained to disown their own identities and use somebody else's memory."

She thought about Grete, who had become an English refugee who sold pictures in a locale down on the second sublevel. She had been infiltrated, so she buried her past and adopted a fictitious one. She was never again able to recall who she had been. Sometimes, in dreams, she made love to a man she did not know. Her true identity had been converted into unconscious material, episodes in the life of a forgotten woman. She was the best photographer in the Museum.

She looked at the world through eyes that were not her own, and this distance showed in her photographs. They had to find her, she could take them to Reyes. The Tano wanted to know who Reyes was.

"He is an ex-professor of English literature who deals in methadone," Elena explained to him. "He is in charge of the clandestine hospitals and the detoxification shelters."

Grete believed that she used to be his wife, a young Englishwoman from Lomas de Zamora who had fallen in love with the young professor who taught courses in E. M. Forster and Virginia Woolf. The story was her alibi, she was a disillusioned woman secretly in love with a man on whom she wanted to take revenge. They had to find her. The cellars of the Mercado del Plata connected to the underground streets that crossed beneath Av. Nueve de Julio and the subway passageways of Carlos Pellegrini Station, where all the subway lines of the city converged. That was a point of escape, a nucleus for refugees and rebels, hippies, gauchos, spies, all sorts of ex's, smugglers, anarchs. To get to the building they had to cross an abandoned parking lot, a no-man's-land between the shelters and the city. They must surely have already seen them in the alleyway and were now watching them on the closed-circuit screens. She saw herself in the Clinic, the white eye of a camera on the ceiling. She thought Arana was speaking with a nurse behind her. She felt she was falling asleep. She was too tired. The Tano took her by the arm and forced her to keep going, almost running between the abandoned parking meters. It was like crossing a forest. The Irish band The Hunger could be heard through the loudspeakers. It was their new anthem, "The Reptile Enclosure." They were the children of the children of the nationalist rebels. At seventeen years of age, Molly Malone was the leader of the band, and she had become a superstar singer with her glassy throat. Her brother Giorgio sang backups with his warm tenor voice, but he would go crazy and change the lyrics, sing rap improvisations over the anthems of the Republican Army. The crowds went mad over Molly Malone's live performances. The concert lasted two hours. The observance personnel had in all likelihood connected their monitors to the broadcasts of channel 9. The Tano thought that luck was on their side and that they might be able to escape. They had one chance in thirty-six. It was always the same. He liked to play roulette because it was a replica of life.

"I'm from Rosario," he said to the Korean guard at the door. "We have to get through. She's a patient of Arana's."

He might be a policeman. Everyone works for the secret services, they all become spies and confidants and legal assassins and policemen who shoot up as part of their undercover work. (In New York half the addicts are detectives.) The more criminal activity found among Asian refugees, the more Asian refugees that the police must recruit as informants. Insanity of resemblance is the law, the Tano thought. To look alike in order to survive. If he was a government agent, he chose not to disclose it. He let them in and guided them to a stairway, and then to a door, and again to a stairway. The white walls and the lighted stained-glass windows created a strange stillness. The music had ceased.

"This is the Museum," the Tano said.

The pavilions extended for kilometers on end, with glass cabinets displaying material from the past. Elena saw a room from a boarding-house in Tribunales, and a man on a low stool strumming a guitar. She saw two gauchos on horseback riding across a line of small fortresses, she saw a man committing suicide on a train seat. She saw a replica of Arana's consulting room, and again her mother's face in the mirror. The Tano hugged her. And this she had also seen. The Tano hugging her in a room of the Museum. She saw the replica of the lighted stage with Molly Malone singing the chorus of "Anna Livia Plurabelle" in a feline voice.

"Let's go," he said, "we have to get out of here."

They came out into a television repair workshop. An old man with white hair and a white beard raised his head from a microprocessor. It was Mac. Elena felt that she was about to cry. The Tano opened the back of a microscopic television set and put it down on the glass counter.

"This apparatus is a family relic," he said, "and I want to keep it running."

"And what is the problem?" asked the man, who spoke with a German accent.

"It only gets channels from the past."

The old man raised his head.

"Everyone wants to be a comedian," he said, and went on connecting the cables of a video recorder that he had to adapt to a closed-circuit.

"She's Elena," the Tano said.

The old man was adjusting the three bands of images, his myopic eyes moving astutely across the microscopic circuits that he himself had designed. He looked at her, but did not recognize her.

"We want to get into the factory," the Tano said.

There was a soft light in the locale, and the rumbling from the subway trains made the ceiling vibrate.

"It's here," the old man said.

A group of scientists had deserted the institutes dedicated to atomic investigation that had been built in the mid-1940s. They started with a small repair shop in an abandoned garage. The factory kept growing quietly, scattered across the desert and the provincial towns.

"We keep in contact," he said. "We are waiting for the right moment to move. There are forty-three of us and we are going to participate in the rebellion." He opened and closed his left hand, as if he were counting the scientists five at a time. "I cannot say anything else. I do not know anyone." He looked at Elena and smiled. Then he spoke to the Tano.

"You can take that apparatus away now, it is fixed. Turn it on."

The tiny images flashed on the screen, and immediately they could see a series of small workshops disseminated across all the towns and small cities of the country. They could see men with white overalls taking apart old radios and rebuilding unused motors.

"What are we going to do?" Elena asked, surprised.

"Nothing," the old man said. "Get out of here."

It was Mac, but he did not know her. She did not go near him, she did not want to touch him, she did not want him to touch her. The world of the dead, Dante's map of the *Inferno*. Circles and circles and circles.

"So then," Arana said, "you are dead and in the *Inferno*. Isn't that smart."

"I used to be smart," Elena said. "Now I'm a machine that repeats stories."

"The one fixed idea," Arana said. He gestured for his assistant. A young doctor wearing a white coat and surgical gloves leaned over Elena and smiled at her with a childlike expression.

"We have to operate," he said. "We have to disactivate her neuro-logically."

"He repairs television sets," Elena said.

"I know," Arana said. "I want names and addresses."

There was a pause. The white glass of the cabinet in the consulting room reflected the spinning fan.

"There's this telepath," Elena said. "He follows me around and reads my thoughts. His name is Luca Lombardo, he's from Rosario, everyone calls him the Tano. If I tell you what you are asking me for, he is going to blow up the microspheres implanted in my heart."

"Don't be stupid," Arana said. "You have become psychotic and are in the middle of a paranoid delirium. We are in a Clinic in the neighborhood of Belgrano, this is an extended drug session, you are Elena Fernández." He stopped and read her chart. "You work in the National Archives, you have two children."

"I am dead, he moved me here, I am a machine."

"We are going to have to use electric shock treatment on her," Arana said to the doctor with the baby face.

"Listen," Elena said. "In the cellars of the Mercado del Plata, in the Korean sector, the one everyone calls Seoul, there is an English pho-tographer, Grete Müller. She works for the rebels." She had to give her up in order to save Mac. Maybe she could warn her before the police showed up. The information had become public. Investigating virtual images, she had found the way to draw pictures of people and things she had never seen.

"We know," Arana said. "I want names and addresses."

Everything was starting over again. The sun rising in the city, the lights of the Mercado del Plata still on. There as well everything was starting over again. In the cellars of the Mercado del Plata, in a lab illuminated with a red light, Grete Müller was developing the photographs that she had taken in the aquarium that night. The patterns on the shells of the turtles were the symbols of a lost language. Originally, the white nodes had been marks on bones. The map of a blind language shared by all living beings. The only traces left of that original language were the patterns on the shells of the sea turtles. Prehistoric shadows and shapes recorded on bone plates. Grete enlarged the photographs and projected them on the wall. The series of patterns were the base of a pictographic language. All the languages of the world had evolved through the centuries from those primitive nuclei. Grete wanted to get to the island, because with this map it would be possible to establish a common language. In the past we all understood the meaning of every word, the white nodes were recorded in the body like a collective memory. She went over to the window high on the wall and looked out over Av. Nueve de Julio. The number of cars declined at that time of the morning, all the activity in the city was nocturnal. Perhaps she would finally be able to sleep and stop dreaming about the Museum and the machine and the proliferation of languages jumbled together to the point of incomprehensibility. They are forgotten worlds, she thought, no one keeps the memory of life anymore. We see the future as if it were the memory of a house from our childhood. She had to get to the island, find the legend of the woman who was going to come and save them. Perhaps, Grete thought, she is lying peacefully on the sand, lost on an empty beach, like a rebellious replica of a future Eve.

III   Mechanical Birds

1

Junior woke up, startled. Once again the phone was ringing at midnight. It was the same woman who mistook him for someone else and told him her ex-husband's sad story. A man she called Mike had gone to Mar del Plata to work as a night watchman in a hotel that was closed down for the winter. He was found dead one morning. They followed the music from the radio from one empty room to another until they finally discovered his body in a dark room with the blinds drawn. The woman said that at first they thought it was a suicide. Then they thought he had been killed by one of the State's secret services. Her ex-husband was on the run, his group was withdrawing in complete disorder, he belonged to the People's Revolutionary Army, a Trotsky-Peronist organization. He was a Trotsky-Peronizt, the woman said, and immediately lowered her voice and began to tell him about the Clinic. She had just spent two months there, she said, in the jail, in the colony. She was rehabilitated, now her name was Julia Gandini. He imagined the woman submerged in a false reality, stuck in someone else's memory, forced to live as if she were another woman. These kinds of stories were circulating throughout the city, the machine had begun to incorporate material from reality. Julia told him that she was not being followed, that she was eighteen years old, that she wanted to see him.

"Even with just half the information I have," she said, "you could run an entire special edition of the newspaper."

She spoke informally to him, as if they were friends, and laughed with a clean, carefree laughter.

They set a time to meet at a bar, at Retiro Station.

"And how will I know you?" she asked.

"I look Russian," Junior told her. "Like Michael Jordan, but white."

"Michael Jordan?" she said.

"The guy who plays for the Chicago Bulls," Junior said. "My face looks just like his."

"I never watch TV," the girl said.

Junior thought that she had been hospitalized and that that was why she did not get the references, as if she lived in a different reality. But he wanted to see her, he did not have too many other alternatives. He had walked through the cellars underneath the Mercado del Plata. He had looked for information in the news cemetery, in the old newspaper archives. He had had dealings in the bars of the Bajo where they sold fake documents, false stories, first editions of the first stories. His room was full of papers, notes, texts pinned up on the walls, diagrams. Recordings. He was trying to find his bearings in the broken plot, to understand why they wanted to disactivate her. Something was out of control. A series of unexpected facts had filtered through, as if the archives were open. She was not revealing secrets, and possibly she did not even know any, but she gave signs of wanting to say something different than what everyone expected. Facts about the Museum and its construction had begun to appear. She was saying something about her own condition. She was not telling her own story, but she was making it possible for it to be reconstructed. That is why they were going to take her out of circulation. She was filtering through real facts. The key was the story of Richter, the Engineer, as Fuyita called him. Junior wanted to make contact, he was certain that the story of the Clinic was a transposition. Maybe the girl could help him make some headway along these lines. Or maybe it was an insignificant fact in a plot with a different meaning. But it was possible she could help him process the information and bring the past up to date. He had spent two nights without sleeping hardly at all since he left the Museum. He was going in and out of the stories, traveling through the city, trying to find his bearings in that plot full of waiting and postponements from which he could no longer escape. It was difficult to believe what he saw, but he was finding the effects in reality, after all. It was like a network, like a subway map. He traveled from one place to the other, crossing stories, moving in several registers at once. And now he was in a bar at Retiro Station, eating a hot dog and drinking beer and waiting for the girl from the phone call to show up. An old man mopped the empty platform. The day's activity was just beginning. Retiro Station was hardly used anymore. The trains to the Tigre Delta ran inconsistently. A woman approached him to ask if the lines were still running. It was six in the morning and the city was just starting to get going, he had to pay attention to all the activity around him without seeming overly anxious. He was watching the subway exit and the main hall. His eyes, like small clandestine cameras, captured the motion of the car that had just stopped to drop off the morning papers at the entrance to one of the platforms. It was the second edition of the day. They did not know what to say. The news continued to accumulate. The patrol cars controlled the city and you had to be very careful to make sure you stayed connected and could follow the events. The control was perpetual. The police always had the last word, they could withdraw his permit to move about the city, they could deny him access to press conferences, they could even withdraw his work permit. It was forbidden to seek out clandestine information. He was counting on Julia, he was waiting for her to show up. Maybe she was telling the truth. Or maybe she would come with a patrol car. There was a strange disparity of consciousness in what was occurring. Everything was normal and yet the danger could be felt in the air, a low alarming murmur, as if the city were about to be bombarded. Everyday life goes on in the middle of the horror, that is what keeps many people sane. The signs of death and terror can be perceived, but there is no clear evidence of behavior being altered. The buses stop at the street corners, the stores are open, couples get married and celebrate, nothing serious can possibly be happening. Heraclitus's sentence has been inverted, Junior thought. He felt as if everyone were dreaming the same dream, but living in separate realities. Certain comments and a certain version of the events made him recall the days of the war over the Islas Malvinas. The Argentine military had lost the war and no one knew it. Women continued to knit jackets and blankets for the draftees in improvised booths in the square by the Obelisk. All certainties are uncertain, Junior ironicized, they have to be lived secretly, like a private religion. It was difficult to make decisions and separate facts from false hopes. He had sat down at a hot-dog stand, under the eaves that face the Plaza de los Ingleses. He was eating a hot dog and drinking a beer and reading the newspaper distractedly. The TV was playing a special program about the Museum. Political trash. The greasy smoke drifted in the air, and yet the place was pleasant. The presence of the drivers at the counter and the cashier in the black coat, who was getting change out of the register just then, cheered Junior up. A man talked to him as if he had known him his whole life. Something had happened with people's sense of reality. The guy was talking with his brother, but there was no brother there.

"The president is an addict and he doesn't even care if people know. Addicts are never embarrassed, because you can't be embarrassed if you don't have any sexual libido," he said.

"Of course," another man said, also sitting at the counter. "Once my wife didn't leave the house for a week because she had a wart this big." He showed everyone the end of his pinkie finger. "A whole week. She didn't want to go out because she said she was disfigured."

"She had tons of sexual libido," the cashier said.

"A whole week without going out."

"And Perón, with all those spots and blotches on his face, to the point where they were calling him 'stain-face.' And he was seen everywhere, he would have himself photographed up close, out in the open, with his leather face."

"When a man has power, if he has it, he wants to be seen."

"Because politics is a mirror," the other man said. "Faces and faces that appear and look at each other and get lost again and are substituted by new faces that appear and look at each other and get lost again."

"It swallows up faces," said the man who had first spoken.

"But the mirror is always there," the other man said, and dropped his head on his arms resting on the counter. "Give me another beer. Do you want another one too, pal?" he asked Junior.

"No, I'm set," Junior said, and at that moment he saw the girl and immediately recognized her. She was coming from the end of the platform and smiled at him at once.

"Now, the truth is," the cashier said, "that television is a mirror."

"Exactly," the other man said. "A mirror that holds onto the faces."

"It has all of them inside and when you look at it you see the other's face."

"That's the beauty of it," the cashier said, growing pensive.

"I'm leaving," Junior said, and set some money down on the counter. "Another round for everyone on me."

There were thank-yous and good-byes as he got up from the stool and walked toward the girl.

They left the train station and walked across to Plaza San Martín. The girl was very attractive, but distant, and she gave off an air of passivity, almost of indifference. As if nothing in the world had any importance. Apathetic. Or maybe afraid, Junior thought. Strange and very beautiful, with a tight Mickey Mouse T-shirt and faded jeans. Right away she began to recite her story. Mike had been wrong and had died because violence only leads to more violence. He lived clandestinely, he commanded several armed operations, he retreated from military activity, moving from one house to another twice a day, until they finally caught him. "In '73 the way I interpreted reality was much more driven by emotions than by political rationale. Today my view of the past is completely different. We were living in the midst of ideological fanaticism. I think the revision needs to be based not only on these last few years, but that it must go back much further. We grew up in a political culture and with a civil conscience both of which were totally wrong. We had to live through this catastrophe in order to learn the value of life and how to respect democracy." She repeated her story like a parrot, in a tone of voice so neutral that it sounded ironic. She had repented. She had attended self-help groups. It was impossible to tell if she was being sincere or if she was schizophrenic. She walked distractedly, every once in a while looking up at Junior.

"Do you find me attractive?" she asked suddenly. She pressed up against him without any warning, and right away moved away, and then walked on, near the wall. The story of her life was the way she had of getting people to love her, immediately she became submissive and started in with her confessions. You could tell she was naive and gullible, but she was not dumb. Frail and pliable, she could have been his daughter.

"Of course," Junior said, and felt a strange emotion stir within him. He had thought about his daughter because it could have been his daughter who had come back, like many others, ten years later. Fourteen years later. But it was not his daughter, and that is why Junior had that strange sensation. It was like an emotion, and yet it had a cold quality, so perhaps it was not an emotion at all. He simply liked to be seen walking with the girl and have people think he was sleeping with her. He was amazed at himself, at how simple everything was. "You escaped from the Clinic," he said to her.

"No one escapes from there," she said. "You go there because you want to, when you can't get off the stuff, then you have to go. There's no such thing as willpower, if you get into it you're lost, it's this stupid thing they've invented to make you kill yourself."

She was not dumb, Junior thought again, only inexperienced. She wanted to help him and told him so right away. She had read Junior's reports, he did not know the whole truth, she had just come from there.

"From where?" Junior asked her.

"Don't be a smart-ass," she said. They had no references in common, everything was simultaneously the same and yet different, as if they spoke two different languages.

76

Junior had to move slowly, let her take the initiative.

"I like it around here," she said after they sat on a bench facing the Círculo Militar. "Enemy territory. See the kinds of places they have, always out of sight, they lock themselves inside those galleries and spend their lives training. I've seen them," she said. "My father was in the military. They practice fencing their whole lives and then shoot you down with real bullets. Do you know how much I'm risking by being here with you?"

"Of course I know," Junior said.

He decided to keep quiet, to let her develop her strategy.

"I'm going to confide in you," she told him. "That's why I called you. Do you know the Engineer?"

"Yes. I mean, they've told me, I've never seen him."

"Do you want to see him?"

"Of course," he said.

"Here," she said to him. "This is for you."

It was an airmail envelope folded in half.

"Don't open it here," she told him. "Put it away, you can open it later."

"I'll put it away," Junior said, and put the envelope in a coat pocket.

"Where do you know him from?" she asked him.

"Everyone talks about him. But I saw the night watchman at the Museum, a Korean guy, Fuyita."

After Junior told her what he knew, she confirmed that the Engineer lived in what was practically a subterranean fortress, that he lived locked up in there, that he was an affable man and very intelligent. He was trapped because the authorities accused him of being irresponsible and criminally insane. They wanted to put him in prison.

"The Engineer never sleeps," she said. "He lives for his experiments. And that's why they say that he's crazy."

Junior wanted to know what the experiments were.

"Verbal," she said. "Proofs of stories about life, versions and documents that people take to him so that he can read and study them."

The Engineer received many letters and phone calls, everyone wanted to interview him. Junior had to hope he would have good luck, and count on the contacts that Julia could get. They were going to enter through a clandestine network while all the foreign correspondents and the official newspapers waited their turn. They had to find a place to hide and wait until tomorrow. She spoke so clearly, in such an indifferent tone, that he ended up believing she was telling the truth. They slept together in a hotel on Tres Sargentos, after eating at the Dorá. Julia seemed simultaneously removed and experienced. She took off all her clothes and hugged him before Junior had finished checking out the room. There was something distant yet real about the girl. Her body was full of scars and she moved skillfully in bed, like a professional pretending to be scared. Junior had to wait for her in the hotel, she told him as she smoked a cigarette, she was going out to get a contact. It was dangerous, but he had to take a risk if he was going to make any progress, and he took the risk. He had let himself get hooked, but he did not regret it. In the morning he was awoken by loud knocks on the door. They said it was a routine inspection. Julia, who came in with the policemen and who had perhaps turned him in, looked at him as if she did not recognize him. He saw her smoking at the window again, as if she had never left. The guys from Narcotics had brought her back. They accused her of dealing and thoroughly searched the room and Junior's clothes.

"You're English," the policeman said.

"My parents were English," Junior responded.

"You worked on the Museum series, for *El Mundo.*"

"I still work there. I can make my sources available to you. Call the newspaper if you want."

"A routine question," the officer said. "Who won the war?"

"Us."

The officer smiled. They wanted to control the principle of reality.

"That's funny. Us who?"

"The Kelpers," Junior said.

The officer enjoyed the answer. Amused, he turned around to one of his assistants. Then he lowered his head and looked at Junior.

"Do you know that this girl is Article 22?"

"Article 22?"

"Street prostitution."

"That's why she was with me," Junior said. "A hundred dollars a night."

"I'd rather not be touched," the girl said when the officer approached her, keeping an absent air about her the whole time. "I make a living my own way, and that's all I care about."

"I won't touch you. Her problem is not political. It's her hallucinations."

A woman cop joined the others now. She was fat and had a face that made her look like an evil character in a TV series, not even a Nazi, something worse, more mechanical, smoother.

"You're ill, child," she said. "You have to go to the hospital. They'll cure you there."

"To which hospital?" the girl asked.

"The neuropsychiatry clinic in Avellaneda."

"Bastards," the girl said. "Let me call a lawyer."

Now that she knew what awaited her, she was in shock. She stood still, withdrawn. Then she leaned against the wall and closed her eyes. She had learned to save her strength and was getting ready to face what she knew she would soon be up against without any illusions.

"She believes in the Engineer, but it's really an illusion. The Engineer died years ago, there is no factory, she can't accept reality. She's psychotic," the officer said. "She's been hospitalized in Santa Lucía since she was seven years old, she's schizo-anarchoid. That man doesn't exist, there's a doctor who she calls the Engineer, there's nothing else to it, it's a clinic. She dreams that she moves around in that marginal world, like a messenger, when in reality she's a prostitute who passes information on to the police."

"Maybe, maybe, maybe," Julia sang out. "He's there, I know it," she said. "When I get out I'll take you."

"See? She has been able to adjust to living out in the real world completely, except for that one fixed idea. It will never disappear, it's indispensable in the balance of her life. But she has to learn to relate to reality, not to a fantasy. And that's what we're here for. To think that there's an internationally renowned physicist hidden in our country. It's an innocuous idea and it helps her survive. But it's false and cannot be propagated. She lives in an imaginary reality," the officer said. "She's at the external phase of the fantasy, an addict running away from herself. She interjects her hallucinations and must be watched." This was the kind of crazy lingo that the police were using now, psychiatric and military at the same time. This was how they intended to counteract the illusory effects created by the machine. Junior remembered his father's ideas about deliriums associated with simulations, and thought that the officer had a removed quality, perverse, as if he thought that simply by being there, alone in his office, he was capable of excluding himself from the world.

"The police," he said, "are completely removed from all the fantasies. We are reality. We are constantly obtaining true confessions and revelations. We care only about real events. We are servants of the truth."

Junior looked at him, but did not say anything.

"We need to verify a few facts," the officer said, "and then we'll let you go."

"And the girl?"

"The girl stays, you go. There always has to be some kind of exchange."

"I don't like it," Junior said.

"I didn't ask you if you liked it, I asked you to tell me your sources."

They made a phone call to the newspaper and immediately released him. He was unable to see Julia. They only allowed him to leave cigarettes and some money for her, although he knew for certain that the same guard who took them would steal them as soon as he left. Junior went out to the street. The buses were heading out toward the city suburbs full of men and women just getting off work. He was at the corner of Paraguay and Maipú. The girl had not turned him in, they had gotten her because of the drugs. The police had not bothered to requisition the papers that she had given him, they had not even opened the envelope. It looked like a blue filing card, with a few facts typed on it. There were a few references to Richter, the Engineer, a German physicist. Then numbers and quotations from several stories, especially from "Stephen Stevensen." That was the point of departure.

2

He spent the next two days alone in his room. He went over the entire series of stories again. There was an implicit message that linked them all together, a message that was being repeated. There was a factory, an island, a German physicist. Allusions to the Museum and to the history of its construction. As if the machine had built its own memory. That was the logic being applied. The events were being directly incorporated, it was no longer a closed system, it was weaving in real facts. She was influenced by other forces — external ones — that entered into the program. Not just situations in the present, Junior thought. It narrates what it knows, it never anticipates. He went back to "Stevensen." It was all there already. The first text demonstrates the process. He had to continue searching along these lines. Investigate what was being repeated. It builds microscopic replicas, virtual doubles, William Wilson, Stephen Stevensen. Once again this same point of departure, a ring at the center of the story. The Museum was circular, like time in the plains. He went back to the story, to the beginning, to the first phrase of the series. "My name is Stephen Stevensen. I am the grandson and great-grandson and great-great-grandson of sailors. My father was the only deserter, and that is why he lived his entire life with the same woman and died a miserable man in a hospital in Dublin. (Stevensen's father had refused to go into the British navy, breaking the very ancient family tradition, and had become an Irish nationalist. His mother's ancestors were Polish. A sarcastic and elegant woman who spent the summers in Málaga, or in the British Museum.) Stevensen was born in Oxford and every language was his mother tongue. Maybe that is why I believed the story he told me, and why I am here, in this lost cattle ranch. But if the story he told me is not true, then Stephen Stevensen is a philosopher and a magician, a clandestine inventor of worlds, like Fourier, or *Macedonio Fernández.*"

Junior was starting to understand. At first the machine would get it wrong. Errors are the first beginning. The machine "spontaneously" breaks up the elements of Poe's story and transforms them into potential fictional nuclei. That is how the initial plot had emerged. The myth of origin. All the stories came from there. The future meaning of what was occurring depended on that story about the other and what is to come. Reality was defined by the possible (and not by what was). The true-false opposition had to be substituted by the possible-impossible opposition. The original manuscript was coiled in a tin cylinder. He was having a hard time reading with his glasses. I am getting more and more myopic every day, Junior thought, moving his face closer to the glass box. It looked like a strip of teletype. "I first arrived here on Wednesday May 4 at three in the afternoon, on a train that was continuing on to Pergamino. I had been invited by the Academia Pampeana and the Jockey Club to spend three months in the large ranch and study the projects of the Scientific Society. I am a doctor (and a writer), I have been in this town for months. I want to meet Doctor Stevensen. He is one of the major English naturalists of the century, Argentine by choice, a descendent of European travelers and researchers who came to these plains to study the habits of the natives. I admired his books, I had read his marvelous *Mechanical Birds,* as well as his biological essays, and his extraordinary *White Voyage.* It has been so long that everything seems unreal to me. But perhaps instead of talking about unreality, I should talk about inexactness. Truth is exact, like the circumference of the crystal glass that measures the time of the stars. The slightest distortion and everything is lost. Lying is no longer an ethical alteration, but rather the failure of a steam engine the size of this fingernail. What I mean to say (Stevensen used to say), is that truth is a microscopic artifact that serves to

83

measure the order of the world with millimetric precision. An optical device, like the porcelain cones that watchmakers adjust on their left eye when taking apart the invisible gears of the very complex instruments that control the artificial rhythms of time. Stephen Stevensen has dedicated his existence to building a miniature replica of the order of the world. As if he wanted to study life in a dry aquarium, the fish opening and closing their mouths in the transparent air for hours on end. He actually decided (I think) that I was part of his experiments and that he would study my reactions. Now I understand that he has been watching me, that he has been observing me ever since I arrived. Or maybe from before, since I took the train in La Plata, and maybe even from the moment I left my house. He lived in the old buildings of the La Blanqueada ranch immediately before me. The morning I arrived he left me the house and moved to the Hotel Colón, with all his papers and machines. He did not return to Buenos Aires, he extended his stay in the town with some sort of trivial excuse (having to do with his sister). Stevensen's invisible presence accompanied me from the very moment I first entered the large house. I felt like someone who enters surreptitiously into the soul of a stranger and rummages in the night trying to discover the stranger's secrets. At first I thought that Stevensen, out of an aristocratic carelessness, had left traces of himself throughout the house. Now I know that it was not out of carelessness. This is a provisional list of the objects I found when I searched the house on the first day."

The story exhibited Stevensen's marks. Junior found the black coat with the leather elbow patches hanging in a closet out in the country. He found a magnifying glass, a train schedule, a monogrammed ring and a bar of sealing wax. On the desk was the draft of the second page of a letter by Stevensen, written in blue ink on a piece of notebook paper: "I like this place, because it has managed to stay just as it was at the precise moment in which it was rebuilt. I feel as if I were living in another time, as if it were the landscape of childhood, but also the abstract and anonymous landscape that old people see in their dreams. The town was completely destroyed in the war." Impressions formed a part of the building of history. It was not possible to adjust to a set time, space was at once uncertain and detailed with minute precision. There was a map of the countryside and a photograph of the station in Necochea. The town was near Quequén, the borders of the large cattle ranch stretched out as far as the sea. On the back wall he saw the photograph of the building, with the covered porch and the water tank. On a counter covered with sand was a replica of the establishment built to scale, with the wire fences and the front gate, the long house, the quarters for the workers, the corrals facing the railroad tracks. If he lifted the wooden roof he could see the layout of the rooms inside the house. A corridor, the adjoining rooms that faced the patio, the kitchen, the long foldout table. On the other wall there was a map of the town, with numbered streets that ended at the port. To the left he saw the dock and the lighthouse, and to the right the wooded road that led to the Hotel Colón. To a side were Stevensen's record player, along with a tape recorder and a radio.

Junior thought about his father, another Englishman lost in the Pampas who collected radio devices and built high-power receivers so he could follow the broadcasts of the BBC. English inventors, railroad engineers, European scientists exiled after the war. Junior went back to the story about Richter, the German physicist who had been invited to come to Argentina by Perón. He was not the only one to whom the story might refer. Many scientists had been working in Argentina since the turn of the century. In the third volume of the *Dictionary of Scientific Biographies* he found the German track he was looking for: "The National University of La Plata, sixty kilometers south of Buenos Aires, has received a large number of European researchers of the highest level since the first decades of the century. Among them, Emil Bosse, the old editor in chief of the journal *Physikalische Zeitschrift;* Bosse's wife, Margrete Heiberg, who undertook her graduate studies at Gotinga; Konrad Simons, a physicist who worked with Planck and Richard Gans, at that time an authority in the field of terrestrial magnetism." He was sure one of them had been Stevensen, he was sure that was the secret name of the Engineer who had worked with Macedonio in the programming of the machine. Junior walked to the window and opened the blinds. Outside, the city. The empty streets, the lights, the subway entrance across the way. He could talk to Hannah. She would help him. When her father had died she had decided to leave behind the academic world—she had once taught philosophy—and transform the bookstore that her grandfather had founded in 1940 into the main center of documentation and reproductions of the Museum of the Novel in Buenos Aires. She had all the series, all the variations, the different editions, and she sold tapes and original stories.

A few suspected that Hannah herself had secret connections with the machine. That she distributed apocryphal stories and false versions, that she was part of the counterinformation groups who sold replicas, copies made in labs mounted in clandestine suburban garages. They had never been able to pin anything on her, but they kept a watch over her and occasionally closed down her business. They wanted to intimidate her, but she continued to fight, because she was proud and rebellious, a queen in the secret court of the city. Junior knew her from before. She was the kind of woman he had always liked, incredibly intelligent and up-front. To see her meant that they would open a file on you, but they already had a file on Junior, and he could not count on receiving legal protection from the newspaper anyway. Better not to let them know he was going to see her, he preferred to move freely as long as he could.

He got out at the Nueve de Julio exit. The corridors were filled with stands and kiosks that sold miniatures and war magazines. Young draftees stopped at the porno shops and the micromovies, the shooting galleries, the cheap bars with pictures of half-naked blondes, the lottery booths. Toward the back there were rickety sheds and locales bunched up along the corridors that took advantage of the continuous traffic of the many people who traveled by subway. With their spiked hair and their torn Levi's, their knives sheathed inside their boots, the youth had invaded the bars. Dressed in tight black city jackets, they made them play heavy metal over the loudspeakers. One of the lateral passages led to a hall that connected directly to an exit. It was like a cone of silence, with a cloudy glare coming down from the street. To one side there was a watchmaker's shop and, across from it, Hannah Lidia's shop. He knocked on the glass door and shortly afterward a light came on inside, in the back. She opened the door in her usual state of relaxed fatalism. She was wearing velvet pants, a man's vest, anticancer bracelets. This time she had her hair up like Prince Valiant, everything was very New Age, total snob mask. She cultivated a slightly psychotic look and was never surprised to see him, even if he had not come by in months. The place had a very tall ceiling and was connected to the subway. It was cold inside. The books were piled up in no particular order whatsoever, and the place gave him an instantaneous feeling of well being. A large photograph of Macedonio Fernández covered the back wall. The room was on the other side of a beaded curtain. A TV on the night table, piles of dirty dishes in a circle around the bed. Two bottles of Black & White on a footstool. She sat on the floor and kept watching TV. She never seemed to grow older. She wore blue contact lenses and had a Museum tattoo on her arm. Junior was glad that she went on living her life without pretending to be interested in him. That she did not ask him what he had been doing, nor how he was, nor where he had been. The last time they saw each other they had kissed next to the stairs, but Hannah had suddenly told him to let go. You're sinking, Junior, she had said to him. He worked at the newspaper, he wrote trash, he was getting cynical. She had not wanted to see him anymore. He had laughed. Who do you think I am? The Titanic? he had answered. We're all sinking, kid. He remembered the woman in the Majestic. It was the same thing. Hannah never left her haunt, either. She went on eating from her plate of ravioli and watching the Mexican channel on TV.

"I read your reports," she said to him. "You're blind."

"Why? It's bait," Junior said. "I print everything. They want to make a little bit of noise at the paper to see if they react."

"They won't react," she said. "They want to take her out of circulation. They are going to close down the Museum." She raised her face from the plate and looked at him with her blue eyes. "Do you know what they are about to do?"

Junior slid his finger across his throat.

"Zip," she said. "They want to stow her away, send her to the museum in Luján. Anything, to get people to forget."

"And they will forget."

"Don't believe it. I've seen several xeroxes of stories from the fifties, versions from the war, science fiction stories. Pure realism."

"Many are apocryphal."

"You're starting to believe what you write," Hannah said.

She was drinking whisky from a small plastic cup. It was three in the afternoon.

"I've been receiving some pretty strange phone calls," Junior said. "I met with a woman at the Hotel Majestic, the other day. Fuyita, you know him? He works in the Museum. A kind of head of security. I went to see him," Junior said. "He passed some material on to me."

"Aha," Hannah said. "You're going to publish it?"

"I don't know," Junior said. "Someone is selling false copies in a shop in Avellaneda. It's a garage on Av. Mitre, they fix tv's, but they're working on the political series."

"I know it," she said.

"Peronists. Ex-Peronists, guys from the Resistance. I'm trying to follow the track that leads to the Engineer."

"Is it true that you're from Bolívar?" she asked suddenly.

"No, I'm not," Junior said. "I lived there for a while, when I was little. Near there, in Del Valle, there was a convent and a school there."

"Aha," Hannah said. "Many are running away to the countryside now. No longer to the south, to the valley, but to the Pampas itself. They put up a shack and plant something, hook up by radio. They move from one place to another. They go around in those shabby old cars and use shortwave receivers. It's hard to find a guy hiding out in the middle of the barren plains. The old vagrants used to do that. Anarchists, philosophers, mystics, when the going got tough and they tried to come down on them, they'd jump a freight car. Vagrants," she continued. "Macedonio was also out in those plains. He carried around a little notebook and was always jotting things down."

She paused and walked to the window. The inside of the bookstore was in the shadows, the bookshelves stood out in the semi-darkness like rusted excavations.

"They want to disactivate her," Hannah said. "They say that they are going to call in the Japanese."

"Japanese technicians, just what we need," Junior said. He imagined them going into the Museum, cutting off the lines of communication, isolating the white hall. They had published a few pictures taken with photoelectric cells. All the tissues were okay. But still, something was dying.

"She has started talking about herself. That is why they want to stop her. We are not dealing with a machine, but with a more complex organism. A system of pure energy. In one of the last stories there is an island, at the end of the world, a kind of linguistic utopia about life in the future. It's a myth," Hannah said, "a fantastic story circulating from hand to hand. A man is shipwrecked and survives and builds an artificial woman with parts that the river washes up on shore. And she stays on the island after he dies, waiting on the shore, mad with loneliness, like a new Robinson Crusoe."

On the screen of the muted TV there was a street with glass buildings, in a city that looked like Tokyo, or perhaps São Paulo. Junior saw billboards written in Spanish and a newspaper stand on a corner. It was Mexico City. Apparently it was a documentary on earthquakes on the west coast.

"Do you know what Macedonio did when Elena died?" Hannah asked after a pause.

"He retired," Junior said.

"Yes, he retired," she said. She would not have told him if he had not said it first.

"I have been following this story for two months, I came here because I want you to help me," Junior said.

"When she got sick, Macedonio decided that he would save her. There are several unaccounted days where no one knows where he was. Apparently he went to a large cattle ranch, in Bolívar. There was an Engineer around there, Russian. You have to follow that track," Hannah told him. "A Hungarian Engineer who had worked with Moholy-Nagy and was one of the major collectors of automatons in Europe. He came here to get away from the Nazis and to look for a mechanical bird. They start pursuing him when Perón falls. That's one track. Look," she said to him, and turned on the projector. Junior saw the portrait of a man with an honest face and small round glasses working in a lab.

"That's him," Hannah said. "The story begins in 1956, in a small town in the province of Buenos Aires."

They say he was seen arriving in town one afternoon in a cart, and that right away they called him the Russian, although he was apparently Hungarian or Czechoslovakian, and when he was drunk he swore that he was born in Montevideo. To make things simpler and not have any problems, people from the countryside call anyone who speaks unusually Russian. He was Russian and his son was named the Russian when he was born. But we are not there yet. First they saw this stranger arrive in the cart and cross the railroad tracks. It was July and the frost was beginning to lift, but he walked around in short sleeves as if it were spring. Around here the Basque Usandivaras used to go out barefoot to milk the cows, winter or summer, but the Russian was unequaled, he never wore winter clothes, he was made for the polar cold, and the frosts of the Province of Buenos Aires did not affect him at all. He was always hot and everyone felt sorry for him, because a man who clashes with the weather looks like he is mad. He had a letter for the intendant, and a long time went by before we learned that he had stolen the letter and the cart from a dead man. The intendant around that time was Ángel Obarrio. He had been appointed by the so-called Liberating Revolution of 1955, and had placed half of the Peronists in Bolívar under arrest, but a week later he had to let them go because there was nobody to look after the animals. It was the winter of '56, the worst one ever. The white air, the puddles in the street like glass. Around then is when the Russian's cart showed up. "Come on. You stupid ass. Shit," he said, but in his language, and shook the reigns, one in each hand, like a gringo. They gave him work at the Federal Shooting Range, and he lived there in a small room out back, near the tub where they cooked up the paste to put up the targets. He mowed the lawn and opened up on weekends when the idiots went down to shoot at the targets. Hardly anybody went during the week, except for the draftees, who came sometimes from Azul, and Doctor Ríos, who had been an Olympic champion in Helsinki and came to train on Tuesdays and Thursdays. The Russian would wait for him, and open the cat-holes of the hall just for him, and watch him prepare his weapons and then raise his left arm and take aim.

They became friends, if you can call it that. Ríos explained to him what the town was like and what he needed to do in order to survive. "Practice target shooting," Ríos would laugh. He did not know that the Russian had killed a man by crushing his skull against the train rails. They had locked him up in the insane asylum because he was unable to make himself understood. He said he had killed the man because of the heat, because it was siesta time and the glare from the sun had blinded him along the railroad tracks. He spent five years at Melchor Romero. Every once in a while he would escape and take off for the hills around Gonnet, but sooner or later he returned to the asylum, thin as a corpse and sick from eating raw birds. Finally he came to this part of the province, following the crops. He was very good with his hands, he was always inventing little devices and taking clocks apart. Ríos was the first one who realized that the Russian was an extraordinary man. Then he wanted to know. He went to the intendant's office and asked to see the letter that the Russian had brought with him. It was a handwritten note from Videla Balaguer, guaranteeing that the man carrying the letter had rendered invaluable services toward the cause of the Liberating Revolution in the glorious days of September 1955. He must have been in the paramilitary units, and that is why Obarrio had assigned him to the Federal Shooting Range. He assumed that he was a man of action and knew his way around weapons. He made a few inquiries. All the facts checked out.

No one told him that the Russian was not Russian, but Hungarian, that he was an engineer who had studied with Moholy-Nagy, that he had come to get away from the Nazis, that he had killed a man, that he had stolen the letter and the cart from a dead man. Ríos had investigated the wrong life. All the facts were true, but it was the wrong man. Ríos laughed, afterward, when he saw all the noise he had stirred up. You can't be a shooting champion and put the bullet right where you put your eye if you don't have the absolute certainty that you are going to hit the bull's-eye every time. Sometimes he missed. But if he missed he would tell himself he had missed on purpose. When events had proved him wrong, and it was already too late, he simply altered the angle of his shot and concentrated on the museum and on Carola Lugo.

"This is a small town," Ríos said. "You always see the same people going around the same places, and yet the hardest thing to understand is precisely what everyone knows. The secret is out in the light and that is why we don't see it. It's like target shooting. It has to do with extreme visibility."

There was a mechanical bird in the town museum. They brought it with the railroads in 1870. It worked to anticipate storms. It would go around in the air, flying out in wider and wider circles, and then head straight toward the water. Even now, when the rain is approaching, it begins to move its wings and jump slightly up and down in the glass cabinet where it is chained up. They have come from Germany to look at it, and they claimed that it was German (that it could not be anything other than a German bird). There is a very old tradition of automatons in the Black Forest, Ríos said. They wanted to buy it, but the bird is a historical piece that belongs to the province, and it is not for sale. The chief of the station, the Englishman McKinley, had lived in the large house where it is kept. His wife abandoned him a week after they got there, and he lived alone ever since. When she saw the Argentine plains, the low weeds, the gauchos with their Japanese faces, the woman went back to Lomas de Zamora, disillusioned. It was McKinley, as strange as it may sound, who became interested in the history of the area, and started gathering mementos. He had belonged to the Royal Geographic Academy in London, and was an honorary member of the British Museum, and would occasionally send them reports about the region. He bought the bird for two hundred pesos from Paul Veterinary's representative. It had been kept for decoration purposes in a cage between the fox terrier puppies and the house parrots. It was invented by a French engineer and used in Argentina to measure the plains when they laid out the tracks of the Ferrocarril del Sur. They would set it free and the animal would fly off, flapping its wings, and disappear into the horizon. When it returned, all they had to do was open a hinge in its chest and take out the clock with the measurements. The Englishman was crazy, he came to build a Museum in this lost little town, in the middle of everybody's indifference. No one was interested in the past here, we all live in the present. If everything has always been the same, forever, what is the use of saving things from a time that has not changed. But McKinley left everything arranged in his will. The municipality took over the house, put a flag above the door, and sometimes, on June 13, which was the anniversary of its foundation, they took the children from the elementary school and performed a ceremony on the sidewalk in front of the building. The Lugos were appointed caretakers, and Carola grew up in that house, playing with all the replicas of the Indian tents and the manes of the embalmed horses when she was a little girl. Sometimes, when some foreign visitor would appear (which occurred every two or three years), they would take the bird out and have it fly and head out toward the rains. One afternoon Ríos took the Russian to visit the museum. The Russian went crazy over the animal. Carola Lugo opened the door for them. She was blond and small and fragile, with a harelip. She showed them the house and the galleries. A different era was represented in each room. There were skeletons and drawings. "The professor was a photographer and could also draw. He made several explorations of the region. In this field that we see over here, near Quequén, he found a cattle ranch in which the gates and the tie beams of the house were made out of whalebone. They probably found the animal on the beach, dead, and thought it would look luxurious to use the skeleton to decorate the countryside. One can just about imagine a country-man, who has never seen a whale in his entire life, go as far as the sea on his horse and find that large mass lying on the sand and think that it is a fish from Hell." The afternoon was freezing and overcast. "Here we see a typical tent. The Indians used this kind of leather to protect themselves against the southern winds." Finally they went through a hallway with photographs and paintings from the laying of the rail-road tracks. The bird was displayed in the center room, inside a glass cabinet. It looked like a vulture and had a fierce gaze and its wings moved as if it were breathing. It was attached by a small chain. Carola opened the glass case and handed it to him. The Russian held it in his two hands, amazed at how little it weighed. Light as the air, he said, and Carola smiled. They went outside to the back patio among the trees. There was nothing but plains and the sky extending end-lessly in every direction. The Russian lifted the bird and gently let it go. At first it flew low to the ground, in circles, with a heavy flap-ping of its wings. Then, suddenly, it faced the storm and took off. It returned after a while, flying back to the patio, moving slowly, and perched itself on Carola's shoulder. The Russian opened its chest and started to explain the clock mechanism that made it work. From that day on the Russian began to go to the museum after he got off work at the Federal Shooting Range. He would stroll through the Indian tents and always end up in the room with the bird. Carola went with him, quietly, peacefully. One night he stayed there, and after that they began living together. He set up a small workshop and started working on a replica of the bird. One morning she was sitting by the door when she saw someone pull up in a Buick. He was looking for the Russian, who had escaped from the insane asylum. He did not resist, he let himself get taken away by the man in the brown suit. The replica of the bird was only halfdone. Now it is on display in a smaller glass cabinet. Its chest is open and the gears and the little clock wheels look like the drawings of a soul. Sometimes it opens its beak, as if it needed more air, and turns its head toward the window. What it has not found is its form, Ríos says, it is suffering from a lack of truth.

3

Junior traveled all night. When he got there he recognized the house as if he had seen it in a dream. The white facade, the tall entranceway, the endless succession of transparent windows. He called at the front door with the bear-claw knocker. The town was empty, the only person he saw was a girl who raised an embroidered curtain and spied out to look at him from behind a window. The old woman who opened the door was Carola Lugo. She looked fragile, and her eyes were hesitant, as if she were blind. She stood to the side, without opening the door all the way. Through the crack Junior saw the long hallway that led to the back of the house. "I have been waiting for you," she said, "Hannah told me you'd be coming." As he entered the thought crossed Junior's mind that he would never be able to leave there, that he would become lost in that woman's story. They walked down a long hallway and into the first room. The tall ceiling and the thin windows gave the house a remote feel to it. Carola gestured as a way of showing him the place, and asked him to take a seat. Junior settled into a long divan while she sat with her back to the window and to an old grandfather's clock.

"The Russian used to live here," she said. "But that is not his name anymore, now he is somebody else, he uses a European name. You have to protect yourself in this country. They come after you because of your past here. I will show you the house now," she said then. "So you can see it."

An empty lot and a wire fence could be seen on the other side of the window. Junior realized that the architecture of the place was strange, as if all the rooms faced a single spot, or as if they were circular. The afternoon was freezing and overcast. At the far end of the room, in a glass cage, there was a monstrous reconstruction of what could be assumed had once been a bird. It was nearly one meter tall and it moved its neck with slow movements. "The bird's madness will stake us out and that will be the last of us," Carola said. The animal was moving around, fluttering, bumping into the bars of the cage. "It's blind," she said. To a side a doll was moving its arms and trying to smile. Junior had the impression that he had seen it before and that it was far too sinister to be artificial. "The Russian was the most important expert in automatons in all of Europe. Look," she said, and opened a wardrobe. They looked like wire insects. "He made them for me, they are the fruits of love. I have spent hours at the train station hoping to see him go by," she said, and smiled. "Me, a seventy-year-old woman."

It was moving to hear her talk. She seemed to be in love with a shadow, with a man who had entered her life for an instant and left her in the past. There was a telescope at one of the windows. Through it you could see the endless plains and the reflection of the small Carhué lake. "The young one moved to Buenos Aires," Carola said, "and I have lived here, alone, in this house, ever since. My brother comes to visit every once in a while, but he is very upset because of everything that has happened." She spoke to him calmly, in a friendly tone, as if Junior were her confidant, the first one who had finally gone there to hear the truth. "They keep me in here by myself because I know the Russian's story. He married me and now I am paying the consequences. They came to get him and he escaped. They wanted him for no reason at all. But he is not dead," Carola said, "he is just hiding on an island in the Tigre Delta. Now he has another name. He is no longer the Russian, or perhaps he is the Russian now and he used a different name before. In any case, the man who came to get him in the Buick was an undercover police agent. In plainclothes, dressed in brown. We have everything recorded. The past lives on. Look, see this map, if you follow this branch of the river here, you

97

will find the island. Do not tell him that you have seen me. You must find him. Macedonio Fernández was always interested in the story of the automatons. That is how they met, when his wife died."

Junior saw the bird in the glass cage again and imagined it flying with a stiff flapping of its wings in the distance. She lived in the middle of all those replicas. A world of madness and mechanical images. "Underneath this room, several hundred feet down, I have discovered two large subterranean caves, old cemeteries of the Indian tribes that lived in this part of the Pampas last century. Those kinds of burial grounds are not that rare in this province, especially in Bolívar. There were large massacres around here. A few old men out in the country still remember." To a side there was a stairwell that led to a basement, illuminated by a dim light. It was a hole reflected in a kaleidoscope, and from there you could see the plains and all the items in the house and the small Carhué lake again. "See that ray of sunlight," Carola said. "It is the eye of the machine. Look," she said to him. In the circle of light he saw the Museum, and in the Museum he saw the machine on the black platform. "Do you know what is going on?"

"Yes," Junior said, "they're replicas."

"They were replicas," she said, "but they have destroyed them." The bird was moving its wings and rubbing its beak. It sounded like dry leaves crackling.

"So then nothing is for certain," Junior said.

She smiled. "Macedonio came to this house, running from the pain of the loss of his wife. Elena died and Macedonio abandoned everything. He joined the Russian and spent some time here. The Russian had a lot of difficulties with the language, his dream was to return to Europe. Macedonio was the only person who understood and spoke to him. They spent many days in this house because Macedonio wanted to be convinced. They walked down a hallway and into a room full of small beveled windows that blocked the outside view. He thought that if he went out to the plains at night, and looked in through the lighted windows, he would see scenes that would help him recover his lost wife. The Russian wanted to build him a world at the level of that illusion, so that he could slowly return to the past. To build him a reality as if it were a house, so that Macedonio could live there. He was so desperate that he had abandoned everything, even his dear little kids, and had come out to the country. He jumped the freight trains heading south with the other vagrants. He lived for a time in the Carril cattle ranch, in the town of 25 de Mayo, and finally came down to Bolívar. He drove a hired car out to the house. They finished the machine out there," she said, and shook her hand toward a shack in the patio.

"At first it was about automatons. The automaton outlasts time, the worst of plagues, the water that wears down stones. Then they discovered the white nodes, the live matter where words were recorded. In the bones the language does not die, it persists through all transformations. I will show you the place where the white nodes have been opened, it is on an island, on a branch of the river, it is inhabited by English and Irish and Russians and other people who have gone there from everywhere in the world, pursued by the authorities, political exiles, their lives threatened. They have been hiding there for years and years, they have built cities and roads along the shores of the island, they have explored the world following the course of the river, and now all the languages of the world have mixed together there, every voice can be heard, no one ever arrives, and if someone does, they do not ever want to leave. Because the dead have taken refuge there. Only one person has come back alive, Boas. He came to report what he had seen in that lost kingdom. Here," she said to him. "Listen, now you will see. Perhaps this story is the road that will take you to the Russian."

The Island

1

We yearn for a more primitive language than our own. Our ancestors speak of an age in which words unfolded with the serenity of the plains. It was possible to follow a course and roam for hours without losing one's way, because language had not yet split and expanded and branched off, to become this river with all the riverbeds of the world, where it is impossible to live because nobody has a homeland. Insomnia is the nation's most serious disease. The rumbling of the voices is continuous, its permutations can be heard night and day. It sounds like a turbine running on the souls of the dead, Old-Man Berenson says. Not wailing, but interminable mutations and lost meanings. Microscopic turns in the heart of the words. Everyone's memory is empty, because everyone always forgets the language in which remembrances are recorded.

2

When we say that language is unstable, we do not mean to imply that there is an awareness of the modifications. You have to leave in order to notice the changes. If you are inside, you think that language is always the same, a kind of living organism that undergoes periodic metamorphoses. The best-known image is of a white bird that changes colors as it flies. The rhythmic flapping of the bird's wings in the transparent air gives off the false illusion of unity in the changing of the hues. The saying is that the bird flies forever in circles because it has lost its left eye and is trying to see the other half of the world. That is why it will never be able to land, Old-Man Berenson says, and laughs with the mug of beer at his mustache again, because it can't find a piece of land on which to set down its right leg. It had to be one-eyed, a tero-bird, to end up on this shitty island. Don't start up, Shem, Tennyson says to him, trying to make himself heard in the noisy bar, between the piano and the voices singing *Three quarks for Muster Mark!*; we still have to go to Pat Duncan's burial, and I don't want to have to take you in a wheelbarrow. That is the meaning of the content of the dialogue—it is repeated like an inside joke every time they are about to leave, but not always in the same language. The scene is repeated, but without realizing it they talk about the one-eyed bird and Pat's burial sometimes in Russian, other times in eighteenth-century French. They say what they want to and they say it again, without the slightest idea that they have used nearly seven languages through the years to laugh at the same joke.

That is how things are on the island.

3

"Language is transformed according to discontinuous cycles that are reproduced in the majority of known languages [Turnbull notes]. The inhabitants can instantaneously talk and understand the new language, but they forget the previous one. The languages that have been identified so far are English, German, Danish, Spanish, Norwegian, Italian, French, Greek, Sanskrit, Gaelic, Latin, Saxon, Russian, Flemish, Polish, Slovenian, and Hungarian. Two of the languages that have appeared are unknown. They shift from one to the other, but are not conceived of as distinct languages, but rather as successive *stages* of one single language." The duration is variable. Sometimes a language lasts for weeks, sometimes just one day. The case of a language that remained still for two years is also remembered. But it was then followed by fifteen modifications within twelve days. We have forgotten the lyrics to all the songs, Berenson said, but not the melodies. Still, there was no way to sing a song. You would see people in the pubs whistling together like Scottish guards, everyone drunk and happy, marking time with mugs of beer while they searched their memories for any words that might go with the music. Melody has survived, it is a breeze that has blown across the island since the beginning of time, but what good is music to us if we can't sing on a Saturday night, in Humphrey Chimpden Earwicker's bar, when we're all drunk and have forgotten that we have to go back to work on Monday.

4

On the island they believe that when old people die they are reincarnated into their grandchildren, this being the reason why one can never find both alive at the same time. However, since, despite everything, it does occur at times, when an old person sees his grandchild, he has to give him a coin before he can talk to him. Historical linguistics is based on this theory of reincarnation. Language is how it is because it accumulates the remnants of the past with each generation and renews the memory of all the dead languages and all the lost ones. He who receives this inheritance can no longer forget the meaning that words had in the days of his ancestors. The explanation is simple, but does not solve the problems posed by reality.

5

The unstable character of language defines life on the island. One never knows what words will be used in the future to name present states. Sometimes letters arrive addressed with symbols that are no longer understood. Sometimes a man and a woman are passionate lovers in one language, and in another they are hostile and barely know each other. Great poets cease being so and see other classics emerge in their own lifetime (which in turn are also forgotten). Every masterpiece lasts only as long as the language in which it is written. Silence is the only thing that persists, clear as water, ever the same.

6

The day's activities begin at sunrise, but if the moon has been out until dawn, the yelling of the youths can be heard from the hillside even before then. Restless in those nights full of spirits, they scream to each other, trying to guess what will happen when the sun rises. Tradition has it that language is modified when there is a full moon, but this belief is belied by the facts. Scientific linguistics holds that there is no correlation between natural phenomena, such as the tide or the winds, and the mutations of language. The men in the town, however, still observe the old rituals, and every night that the moon is full they stay up, waiting for their mother tongue to finally arrive.

7

On the island they cannot picture, they cannot imagine, what is outside. The category of a "foreigner" is unstable. How they conceive of their homeland depends on the language spoken at any given point in time. ("The nation is a linguistic concept.") Individuals belong to the language that everyone spoke when they were born, but no one knows when that particular language will return again. "That is how something emerges in the world [Boas has been told] that appears to everyone in childhood, but where no one has ever been: the homeland." They define space in relation to the Liffey River that runs through the island from north to south. But Liffey is also the name of the language, and all the rivers of the world are in the Liffey River. The concept of borders is temporal, their limits conjugated like the tenses of a verb.

8

We are now in Edemberry Dubblenn DC, the guide said, the capital that combines three cities in one. Currently the city runs from east to west, following the left bank of the Liffey through the Japanese and West Indian neighborhoods and ghettos, from the origin of the river in Wiclow to Island Bridge, a little below Chapelizod, where it continues its course. The next city appears as if it were built out of potentiality, always in the future, with iron streets and solar energy lights and disactivated androids in the cells of Scotland Yard. The buildings emerge from the fog, without any set shape, sharp, shifting, almost exclusively populated by women and mutants.

On the other side, to the west, above the area of the port, is the old city. When you look at the map you have to keep in mind that the scale is drawn according to the average speed of walking a kilometer and a half per hour on foot. A man comes out of 7 Eccles Street at eight in the morning, goes up Westland Row. On each side of the cobblestones are the gutters that lead to the shores of the river, where the singing of the washerwomen can be heard. A man going up the steep street toward Baerney Kiernam's tavern tries not to hear the singing, hits the gratings of the cellars with his walking stick. Every time he turns onto a new street, the voices grow older. It is as if the ancient words were engraved on the walls of the buildings in ruins. The mutation has overwhelmed the exterior shapes of reality. "That which still isn't defines the architecture of the world," the man thinks, and goes down to the beach around the bay. "You see it there, on the edge of language, like the memory of one's house from childhood."

9

Linguistics is the most advanced science on the island. For generations scholars and researchers have worked on a project to develop a dictionary that would include future variations of known words. They would need to establish a bilingual lexicon that would allow for the comparison of one language with another. Imagine (Boas's report says) an English traveler who arrives in a new country. In the hall of the train station, lost in the middle of a foreign crowd, he stops to check a small pocket dictionary for the right phrase. But translation is impossible, because the only thing that defines meaning is usage, and on the island they never know more than one language at a time. By now, those who still persist in trying to develop the dictionary think of it as a divination manual. A new Book of Mutations,

Boas explained, conceived as an etymological dictionary containing the history of the future of the language.

There is only one known case in the history of the island of a man who knew two languages at the same time. His name was Bob Mulligan, and he claimed that he dreamt incomprehensible words whose meanings were transparent to him. He spoke like a mystic and wrote foreign phrases and said that those were the words of the future. A few fragments of his texts have survived in the Archives of the Academy, and one can even listen to a recording of Mulligan's high-pitched, mad voice as he tells a story that begins like this: "Oh New York city, yes, yes, the city of New York, the whole family has gone there. The boat was full of lice so they had to burn the sheets and bathe the children in water mixed with acaricide. The babies had to be separated from each other, because the smell made them cry if they smelled it on each other. The women wore silk handkerchiefs over their faces, just like Bedouins, although they were all redheads. The grandfather of the grandfather was a policeman in Brooklyn who had once shot and killed a gimp who was about to slice the throat of a supermarket cashier." No one understood what he was saying. Mulligan wrote the story down, as well as several others, in that unknown language, but then one day he announced that he could not hear anymore. He would come to the bar and sit there, at that end of the counter, drinking beer, deaf as a post, and he would get drunk slowly, with the facial expression of someone who is embarrassed to have made himself noticed. Never again did he want to talk about what he had said. He lived the rest of his life somewhat removed, until he died of cancer at the age of fifty. Poor Bob Mulligan, Berenson said, when he was young he was a sociable guy, and very popular. He married Belle Blue Boylan, and a year later she died, drowned in the river. Her naked body showed up on the east bank of the Liffey, on the other shore. Mulligan never recovered, nor married again. He lived the rest of his life alone. He worked as a linotypist at the Congressional presses, and he would come with us to the bar, and he liked betting on horses, and then one afternoon he started telling those stories that no one understood. I believe, Old-Man Berenson said, that Belle Blue Boylan was the most beautiful woman in all of Dublin.

All attempts to create an artificial language have been derailed by the temporality of the structure of experience. They have been unable to construct a language that is outside the island, because they *cannot imagine* a system of signs that could survive through time without undergoing any mutations. The statement *a* + *b equals c* is only valid for a certain amount of time, because in the irregular space of just two seconds *a* becomes -*a* and the equation changes. Evidence is only good for the length of time it takes to formulate a proposition. On the island, being fast is a category of truth. Under these conditions, the linguists of the Area-Beta of Trinity College have achieved something that should have been all but impossible: they have *almost* been able to root the uncertain form of reality within a logical paradigm. They have defined a system of signs whose notation changes with time. That is to say, they have invented a language that expresses what the world is like, but is unable to name it. We have been able to establish a unified field, they told Boas, now all we need is for reality to incorporate some of our hypotheses into the language.

They know that there have been seventeen cycles to date, but they believe that potentially there must be a nearly infinite number, calculated at eight hundred and three (because eight hundred and three is the number of known languages in the world). If in almost a hundred years, since the changes began to be recorded in 1939, seventeen different forms have been identified, then the most optimistic believe that the full circle could be completed in as little as twelve more years. No calculation is certain, however, because the irregular duration of the cycles is part of the structure of the language. There are slow times and fast times, just like the different stretches of the Liffey. As the saying goes, the lucky ones sail in calm waters, and the best ones live in fast times, where meaning lasts as long as a rooster's bad mood.

But the more radical youth of the *Trickster* group at the Area-Beta of Trinity College laugh at these silly old sayings. They think that as long as language does not find the borders that contain it, the world will be nothing more than a set of ruins, and the truth is like fish gasping for air as they die in the mud when the level of the Liffey recedes in the summer droughts, when the river becomes nothing more than a small, dark-watered rivulet.

10

I said earlier that tradition has it that the ancestors speak of a time in which language was an open field, where one could walk without finding any surprises. The different generations, the elders argue, used to inherit the same names for the same things, and they could leave written documents behind with the certainty that everything they wrote would be legible in times to come. Some repeat (without understanding it) a fragment of that original language that has survived through the years. Boas says that he heard the text recited as if it were a series of drunkards' jokes, the pronunciation thick and pasty, the words broken up by laughter and other sounds that no one knew any longer if they formed part of the original meaning or not. Boas says that the fragment called *Regarding the serpent* went like this: "The season of the strong winds has arrived. She feels that her brain is torn out of her and that her body is made out of tubes and electrical connections. She talks nonstop and sometimes sings and says she can read my mind and asks only that I be near her and not abandon her on the sand. She says that she is Eve and that the serpent is Eve and that no one in all these centuries and centuries has dared to utter this pure truth and that the only one who said it was Mary Magdalene to Christ before she washed his feet. Eve is the serpent, the endless mutation, and Adam is alone, he has always been alone. She says that God is the woman and that Eve is the serpent. That the tree of knowledge is the tree of language. They only start talking once they eat the apple. That is what she says when she is not singing." For many this is a religious text, a fragment from Genesis. For others it is only a prayer that has survived the permutations of language in people's memory, and has been remembered as a game of divination. (The historians assert that it is a paragraph from the letter that Nolan left before killing himself.)

II

A few geneaological sects maintain that the first inhabitants of the island were exiles who were carried there by the rising river. Tradition speaks of two hundred families confined in a multiracial camp in the slums of Dalkey, north of Dublin, who were rounded up and held in the anarchist neighborhoods and suburban areas of Trieste, Tokyo, Mexico City, Petergrad.

Aboard the *Rosevean,* a three-mast ship, with a Pohl-A-type propeller, in the north bay, according to Tennyson, they were carried backward in time on the river, by the freezing gusts of the January winds.

The experiment of confining exiles to an island had already been utilized before as a way to confront political rebellions, but it had always been used with isolated individuals, especially to repress leaders. The best-known case is that of Nolan, a militant of a Gaelic-Celtic resistance group who infiltrated the queen's cabinet and became Möler's right-hand man in the propaganda planning campaign. He was uncovered because he used meteorological reports to encode messages to the Irish ghettos in Oslo and Copenhagen. History recounts that Nolan was found out by chance, when a scientist from MIT in Boston used a computer to process the messages emitted by the meteorological office in the span of a year, with the intention of studying the infinitesimal weather changes of Eastern Europe. Nolan was exiled. He reached the island after drifting randomly for nearly six days, and then lived completely alone for almost five years, until he committed suicide. His odyssey is one of the greatest legends in the history of the island. Only a stubborn, Irish son-of-a-bitch could have survived that long by himself like a rat in this vastness, singing *Three quarks for Muster Mark!* against the waves, screaming it out loud, on the beach, always looking in the sand for the footprint of another human being, Old-Man Berenson said. Only a man like Jim could have built a woman to talk to during those endless years of solitude.

The myth says that he built a two-way recorder with the remnants from the shipwreck, and that with this he was able to improvise conversations using Wittgenstein's linguistic games. His own words were stored by the tapes and reelaborated as responses to specific questions. He programmed it so he could speak to a woman, and he spoke to it in all the languages he knew, and at the end it became possible to believe that the woman had even fallen in love with Nolan. (He, for his part, had loved her from the very first day, because he thought that she was the wife of his friend Italo Svevo, the most beautiful madonna of Trieste, with that gorgeous red hair that reminded you of all the rivers of the world.)

After being on the island for three years, the conversations began to repeat cyclically, and Nolan became bored. The recorder started mixing up the words ("Heremon, nolens, nolens, brood our pensies, brume in brume," it would say, for example), and Nolan would ask "What? What did you say?" It was around that time that he began calling her Anna Livia Plurabelle. At the end of the sixth year of exile, Nolan lost all hope of being rescued. He could no longer sleep properly, and he began having hallucinations, and dreaming that he was awake all night long, listening to the sweet, wireless whispers of Anna Livia's voice.

He had a cat, but when the cat went up the hillside one afternoon and did not return, Nolan wrote a farewell letter, set his right elbow down on the table so his hand would not shake, and shot himself in the head. The first people from the *Rosevean* who went onshore found the voice of the woman still talking from the bifocal recorder. She barely mixed the languages, according to Boas, and it was possible to understand perfectly the desperation that Nolan's suicide had produced in her. She was on a rock, facing the bay, made out of wires and red tapes, lamenting Nolan's death in a soft metallic murmur.

I have woven and unwoven the plotlines of time, she said, but he has left and will not be back. A body is a body, but only voices are capable of love. I have been here alone for years, on the banks of every river, waiting for night to arrive. It is always daytime, at this latitude everything is so slow, night never arrives, it is always daytime, the sun goes down so slowly, I am blind, out in the sun, I want to tear off "the iron blindfold" from my head, I want to bring "the concentrated darkness of Africa" here. Life is always threatened by hunters (Nolan has said), it is necessary to build meaning *instinctively,* like the bees their honeycombs. Unable to ponder my own enigma, I conclude that he is not the one narrating, but rather his Muse, his universal song.

12

If the legend is true, the island was a large settlement for exiles during the period of the political repression following the IRA counteroffensive and the fall of the Pulp-KO. But there is no historian who knows the least bit about that past or about the time when Anna Livia was alone on the shore or about the time when the two hundred families arrived. There are no traces left attesting to any of these events. The only written source available on the island is *Finnegans Wake,* which everyone considers a sacred text, because they can always read it, regardless of the stage of language in which they find themselves.

In fact, the only book that lasts in this language is the *Wake,* Boas said, because it is written in all languages at once. It reproduces the permutations of language on a microscopic scale. It is like a miniature model of the world. Through the course of time it has been read as a magical text containing the keys to the universe, and also as the history of origin, and the evolution of life on the island.

No one knows who wrote it, nor how it got here. No one remembers if it was written on the island, or if it was brought on shore by the first exiles. Boas saw the copy that is kept in the Museum, in a glass box, suspended in nuclear light. A very old edition printed by Faber & Faber, over three hundred years old, with hand-written notes in the margins, and a calendar with a list of the deaths of an Irish family in the twentieth century. This was the copy used to make all the other copies that circulate on the island.

Many believe that *Finnegans Wake* is a book of funereal ceremonies and study it as the founding text of the island's religion. The *Wake* is read in churches like a Bible, and is used for sermons in every language by Presbyterian ministers and Catholic priests. Genesis tells of a curse from God that led to the Fall and transformed language into the rough landscape it is today. Drunk, Tim Finnegan fell into the basement down a flight of stairs, which immediately went from *ladder* to *latter* and *latter* led to *litter* and with all the confusion became the *letter,* the divine message. The letter is found in a pile of trash by a pecking chicken. Signed with a tea stain, the text has been damaged by the long time it has remained in the trash. It has holes and blurred sections and is so difficult to interpret that scholars and priests conjecture in vain about the true meaning of the Word of God. The letter appears to be written in all languages at once and continually changes under the eyes of men. That is the gospel and the garbage dump whence the world comes.

The commentaries of *Finnegans Wake* define the ideological tradition of the island. The book is like a map, and history is transformed depending on the course chosen. The interpretations multiply and the *Wake* changes as the world changes, and no one imagines that the life of the book might cease. However, in the flow of the Liffey there is a recurrence of Jim Nolan and Anna Livia, alone on the island, before the last letter. That is the first nucleus, the myth of origin precisely as it is told by the informants (according to Boas).

In other versions, the book is the transcription of Anna Livia Plurabelle's message. Her reading her husband's (Nolan's) thoughts, and speaking to him after he is dead (or asleep), the only one on the island for years, abandoned on a rock, with the red tapes and the cables and the metallic frame in the sun, whispering on the beach until the two hundred families arrive.

13

All the myths end there, and so does this report. I left the island two months ago, Boas said, and I can still hear the music of that language that flows like a river. They say there that he who hears the song of the washerwomen at the shores of the Liffey will not be able to leave. I, for my part, have not been able to resist the sweetness of Anna Livia's voice. That is why I will be returning to the city that exists in three times at once, and to the bay where Bob Mulligan's wife lies, and to the Museum of the Novel where *Finnegans Wake* is found, alone in a room, in a black glass box. I, too, will sing in Humphrey Earwicker's tavern—drinking beer and pounding on the wooden table with my fist—a song about a one-eyed bird that flies endlessly above the island.

IV ON SHORE

1

Following the turns of the channels and the tributaries of the major waterways of the Delta that borders the city, with its islands and streams and waterlogged lands, was like looking at the chart of a lost continent. Junior had a map, and when he arrived at the Tigre he asked around and was shown the route at one of the terminals of the Inter-Islander. He hired a pilot from the station and rented a motor launch at the Rowing Club. If his calculations were correct, the Russian's colony should be off of one of the bends of the Pajarito, before reaching the open river. They had to navigate up the Carapachay and come out along the stronger currents of the northern waterways. The further he went up the Paraná de las Palmas, the more and more secure Junior felt, as if he were crossing a border that was taking him back to the past—and somehow, strangely, bringing him closer to his daughter. After traveling for two hours, the vegetation became denser, and they passed the remains of a laboratory, indicating that they were approaching the Russian's plant. They skirted an islet full of rushes, then a sandbank, and came out again into open waters. Up ahead, hazily in the fog, he could see higher ground, with jagged ravines and cement foundations. In the middle, elevated on stone pillars and surrounded by an iron railing, was a fortified building with broad circular windows facing the gardens and the river. A man on the dock waved his hat at them, motioning for them to moor there. He was one of the Russian's assistants. He welcomed Junior and helped him off the motor launch, holding his arm firmly, and showed him the path up to the house. The building was in the middle of a clearing. A pebbled path crossed through a small forest of willow trees and led right up to the wire fence surrounding the house.

"Santa Marta Island, and on this side is the Biguá creek. This area has always been occupied by foreigners," the man explained to him. He seemed friendly and obliging, and spoke with a slight accent that sounded like a speech defect. They went through the gate and climbed toward the gardens. At that moment, a tall, thin man was seen walking across the gardens toward them with his hand extended.

"I am the Russian. You are the journalist, and I must ask you to be discreet and not take any photographs. Come, sit here," he showed him a wicker chair on the veranda that surrounded the house. "They think," he said, "that they have disactivated her, but that is not possible, she is alive, she is a body that expands and retreats and captures what is going on. Look," he said, "there is a faucet out there in the garden, almost at ground level, and very cool, clean, crisp water comes out of it, even in the middle of summer. It is at the foot of those hedges over there. Sometimes I imagine that I go over and lie face up on the grass, to drink. But I never go, so I keep a certain possible action alive. Do you see what I mean? An open option, that is the logic of experience, always what is possible, what is to come, a street in the future, a door in a boardinghouse by Tribunales, near the courthouse, and the strumming of a guitar. There is no such thing as an imperfection, in reality it has to do with stages, the third stage or the third area, as was foreseen. There has been a retreat, a strategic withdrawal." "We," the Engineer said, "have reached a point in which we are able to conceive of life as a mechanism whose most important functions are easily understood and reproduced, a mechanism that we can make run at faster or slower rhythms, and thus at a higher or lower intensity. A story is nothing more than a reproduction of the order of the world on a purely verbal scale. A replica of life, if life consisted just of words. But life does not consist just of words. Unfortunately, it is also made up of bodies or, in other words, of disease, pain, and death, as Macedonio would say.

"Physics develops so quickly," he said all of a sudden, "that within six months all knowledge is outdated. They become hallucinations, forms that spring forth from memory. The moment you remember them, they are already lost."

He had had a serious illness and had stopped pretending he was European, and from the moment he became a naturalized citizen everyone started thinking that he was an Austrian, Hungarian, or German who pretended he was from Argentina, and they made him out to be a Nazi physicist hiding in the Tigre, an assistant of Von Braun, a disciple of Heidelberg. "You should not try to be one thing so that people will think that you are something else, if you know what I mean. If you are an anarchist, then be an anarchist, and they will assume that you are an undercover policeman and you will never get caught. If you are who you truly are, then everyone believes you are somebody else." He even knew quite well that it was now being said that he was really Richter, the atomic physicist who had tricked General Perón by selling him the secret to make an atom bomb in Argentina. "But no," he said, "I am the Russian." He had studied Richter's personality because he was amused by the deception he had been able to pull off, "a true virtuoso job," but he was the Russian, an Argentine inventor who made a living selling small practical devices, cheap patents of simple machines that helped improve demand in hardware and general grocery stores in small towns.

"Look at this, for example," he said, and showed him a pocket watch. Then he opened it, wound it up, and the face became a magnetic chessboard with microscopic pieces that were reflected and amplified by a magnifying mirror on the concave glass top. "It is the first chess-playing machine designed in Argentina," the Russian said. "In La Plata, to be precise. It uses the gears and the small clock wheels to program its moves. The hours are its memory. It has twelve options per move, and it was with this very apparatus that I defeated Larse the time he came to play in the Masters Tournament in Mar del Plata, in 1959." He pressed a button on one of the wheels, and the clock became a clock again. "Inventing a machine is easy, as long as you can modify the parts of a previous mechanism. The possibilities of converting what already exists into something else are infinite. But I would not be able to make something out of nothing. In that respect, I am not like Richter. You cannot compare my discovery with Richter's invention, he built an atomic plant for Perón using only words, just with the reality of his German accent. He told him he was an atomic scientist and that he had the secret to make the bomb, and Perón believed him and fell like a fool, and had underground buildings and useless labs with pipes and turbines built for him that were never used. Perón would stroll through the marvelously decorated facilities while Richter, with a strong German accent, explained his wild plans of how he would produce nuclear fission in a cold environment. He won him over with his story, he was just a poor high school physics teacher, and he was not even German, he was actually Swiss, and Perón, who spent his life surpassing everyone, who spent his time nudging and winking and saying things with double meanings, believed Richter's fantastic story and defended it to the end. After all, though, it is the same thing, I mean, for Macedonio that was the basic principle to building the machine. The fiction of a German accent. Everything is possible, all you have to do is find the right words. When he found me, he immediately convinced me that we should start working together.

"Look," he said, "politicians believe scientists (Perón–Richter), and scientists believe novelists (the Russian–Macedonio Fernández). Scientists are big readers of novels, the last representatives of a nineteenth-century public, the only ones who really consider the uncertainty of reality and the form of a story. Physicists, Macedonio would say, added the *quarks* to the basic particle of the universe, in homage to Joyce's *Finnegans Wake*. The only friend Einstein had at Princeton, his only confidant, was the novelist Hermann Broch, whose books, especially *The Death of Virgil*, he could quote from memory. The rest of the world spends its time believing superstitions on television. The criteria of reality," the Russian said, "has crystallized and become concentrated, and that is why they want to deactivate the machine.

I am sure you know the story of the Japanese soldier who stayed in the jungle fighting the American army for thirty years without surrendering. He was convinced that the war was eternal, that he had to avoid getting ambushed and keep moving constantly through the island until he made contact with his own forces. He grew old as he roamed around, eating lizards and weeds, sleeping in a straw hut, climbing up a tree during the typhoon season and tying himself to the branches. The fact of the matter is that that is how war is, and the soldier was only doing his duty, and, except for a nearly microscopic detail (the signatures on a piece of paper declaring peace), his entire universe was real. When they found him he did not know how to speak anymore, he just repeated the oath of the Imperial Army in which he swore to fight to the end. Now he is a ninety-year-old man, exhibited in the Museum of the Second World War, in Hiroshima, dressed in his threadbare officer's uniform of the emperor's army, holding a rifle with a bayonet at waist level, in fighting stance.

"Macedonio captured very clearly the direction of the new situation. If politicians believe scientists, and scientists believe novelists, then the conclusion was simple. It was necessary to effect reality and use scientific methods to invent a world in which it is not possible to have a soldier who spends thirty years in a jungle following orders, or at least a world in which the soldier no longer serves as an example of conviction and a sense of duty that is reproduced by Japanese executives and workers and technicians who are living the same fiction today, on a different scale, and who are always presented as the representatives of modern man. Macedonio's main enemy was the Japanese model of feudal suicide, with its paranoid politeness and its Zen conformity. They build electronic devices and electronic personalities and electronic fictions and in every State of the world there is a Japanese brain giving orders. The State intelligence is essentially a technical mechanism designed to alter the criteria of reality. We have to resist. We are trying to build a microscopic replica, a female defense machine, against the experiences and the experiments and the lies of the State.

"Look," he said, and raised his hand in a gesture that encompassed the trees and the nearby islands, "there are microphones and cameras and policemen hidden everywhere, they watch and record us around the clock. I do not even know if you yourself are a journalist or a spy, or both things at once. It does not matter, I have nothing to hide, they know where I am, and if they do not come it is because I am already outside the law. The State knows all the stories of all the citizens, and retranslates them into new stories that are then told by the president of the republic and his ministers. Torture is the culmination of that desire to know, the maximum degree of institutional intelligence. That is how the State thinks, and why the police mainly torture the poor, only the poor or the workers or the dispossessed, who you can see are darker-skinned or mestizos, they are tortured by the police and by the military. Only in very exceptional cases have they tortured people belonging to other social classes, and these cases have always become major scandals, like when Bravo, the student, was tortured by Amoresano and Lombilla in the time of General Perón. Because when they decide to torture people of slightly higher social standing, it always leads to a scandal, and in the last few years, in which the Army has acted with a homicidal and paranoid rancor, and men, women, and children belonging to distinguished spheres of society have been tortured and brutalized, everything has been denounced and has become known. And even if, of course, the largest number of those killed were workers and peasants, they have also executed priests, landowners, industrialists, students, and at the end they had to retreat before international pressure, which accepts as a given that the humble from the fields, the wretched and feverish from the ghettos and the poorest neighborhoods of the city will be massacred and tortured, but reacts when intellectuals and politicians and the children of well-to-do families are treated this way. Because, in general, the latter already collaborate of their own accord and serve as an example and adapt their lives to the criteria of reality established by the State, without there being any need to torture them. The others would do the same, but they cannot because they have been leveled and cornered, and even if they wanted to and took great pains to that end, they can no longer act like the model Japanese citizen who works fifteen hours per day and always greets the general manager of his company with the slightest of nods. They control everything, they have founded the mental State," the Russian said, "which is a new stage in the history of institutions. The mental State, the imagined reality, we all think like they do and imagine what they want us to imagine.

"That is why I like how Richter infiltrated the Argentine State, he infiltrated his own paranoid imagination into Perón's paranoid imagination by selling him the secret of the atom bomb. Only the secret, because the bomb never existed—only the secret, which, since it was a secret, could not be revealed. Of course, now, after years and years of systematic torture, of concentration camps designed to make those who have repented perform informational duties, they have won everywhere and can no longer be infiltrated, and the only thing that can be done is to create a white node and start over again. There is nothing left, nothing at all, just us, to resist—my mother and I, on this island—and Macedonio's machine. It has been fifteen years since the Berlin Wall fell, and the only thing left is the machine, and the machine's memory. There is nothing else, do you understand what I am saying, young man?" the Russian asked. "Nothing, just the stubble, the dry plains, the marks from the frost. That is why they want to deactivate her.

"At first, when they realized they could not just ignore her, when it became known that even Borges's stories came from Macedonio's machine, and that there were new versions going around about what had happened with the Islas Malvinas, they decided to take her to the Museum, to invent a Museum for her. They bought the building from the RCO and placed her there, on exhibit, in a special gallery, to see if they could negate her, convert her into what is known as a museum piece, a dead world, but the stories were reproduced everywhere, they could not stop her, there were stories and stories and more stories. Do you know how it all began? I will tell you. It always begins the same way, the narrator is sitting down, like I am, on a wicker chair, he rocks back and forth, looking out at the flowing river, it has always been like this, from the beginning, there is someone on the other side waiting, someone who wants to know what happens next. I had a small workshop in Azul around that time, I had lost my position at the Astronomical Observatory in La Plata for political reasons and had installed a workshop to repair radio and television sets. I was already carrying out my investigations, at night, I had begun to combine certain formulas together, to do some calculations, nothing too specific, around the time when Gödel's and Tarski's hypotheses first began to be disseminated. I applied them to a radio receiver, I was unable to build a transmitter, not at that point, just a recorder, my closet was full of tapes, recorded voices, lyrics, I was not able to transmit, only to capture, from the ether, waves, memories. I insist that at this point Gödel's work had just appeared, around the same time as Tauski's essay, I was in contact with the Rodríguez Bookstore in Buenos Aires, and I would get the latest scientific and philosophical books and journals every two months, in German, in English. I would work on my investigations at night and open up the electrical repair shop in the morning, until one day this man appears, a poet and a philosopher, I should say, he came to speak with me because everyone knows everything in small towns and he had been told that there was a European mathematician, he had come to spend some time at the small Arteaga farm, which was nearby, and was told that there was a German, because everyone always thought that I was German or Russian, and he wanted to meet me. That is how everything began. He had started before, actually, with other kinds of experiments, but along the same line.

"I remember a friend of mine, Gabriel del Mazo, who knew him from when they were young. I remember hearing him say that one day he was in the living room in Macedonio's house, at 2120 Piedad Alley, parallel to Av. Bartolomé Mitre. It was a big house that is still there, with a patio and a yard with grapevines. They used to meet there with Juan B. Justo and Cosme Mariño, the founders of the Socialist Party and the Anarchist Movement in Argentina, and Gabriel del Mazo remembered that Macedonio was still single and that, one day, he heard the strumming of chords on a guitar ceaselessly from the room next door, the strumming of the chords, Del Mazo said, keeping rhythm in long intervals with other chords, and others, and others and with nothing else. I was intrigued, he says, so I go and ask him what he's doing. And he told me something that I fear I won't be able to recount exactly because my memory is not that great, Macedonio does, Del Mazo says, but it went something like this:

" 'That it is very interesting to look for the fundamental chords in music from which, perhaps, the entire universe is derived.'

"As if he were searching for a kind of primordial cell, the white node, the origin of forms and words, in the strumming of a guitar, in the melody that is repeated and repeated and repeated and never ends. A nucleus that is the origin of all voices and of all stories, a common language, as if it were recorded in the flight of birds, on the shells of tortoises, a unique form. You might say that, metaphysically, he did not distinguish dreams from reality. His theory consisted of not differentiating between being awake and dreaming. Despite the objective appearance of reality, he opposed it with dreams. He did not believe that dreams were an interruption of the real, but rather an entranceway. You awake from one dream and into another life. The intersection is always unexpected, life is a woven tapestry that interweaves one dream with another. He thought that the self, when it dreams, lives with so much intensity that it experiences as much as, if not more than, when it is awake and its eyes are wide open. All his work revolved around this node. He has written on the subject. That which is not defines the universe as much as that which is. Macedonio placed the possible within the realm of the real. That is why we started discussing Gödel's hypotheses. A formal system cannot attest to its own cohesion. That was our point of departure, virtual reality, worlds of possibility. Gödel's theorem and Alfred Tarski's treatise on the borders of the universe, the outer limits. Macedonio had a very clear awareness of the intersection, the shore beyond which something else begins. That is why when his wife died, it also became necessary for him to leave his life behind, that he too abandon his life, as she had abandoned hers, as if he had gone to find her and she was on the other shore, on what Macedonio called the other shore. He became a shipwrecked man carrying a box with what he had managed to save from the water. He lived in an imaginary island, in complete loneliness, for years and years, like Robinson Crusoe.

"When his wife died he abandoned everything, his children, his legal title, even his writings on medicine and philosophy, and began to live without anything, almost like a vagrant on the road, with other anarchists who were hopping freight trains around that time, out in the country, under bridges, eating only soup, broth made from thistles, sparrow bones. Because he was an extremely ascetic person, no matter how much he had of something it was always more than what he needed, even if he did not have something it was still more than what he needed. He walked alone, played his guitar in small bars in the Province of Buenos Aires, carrying Elena's soul, as he would say, in a small container usually used to carry *mate*. In other words, it contained the letters and the one photograph he had of her wrapped up in strips of cloth. He had discovered the existence of the verbal nuclei that keep remembrances alive, words they had used that brought all the pain back into his memory. He was removing them from his vocabulary, trying to suppress them, and establish a private language without any memories attached to it. A personal language, without memories, he wrote and spoke English and German, so he would mix the languages, in order to avoid even grazing the skin of the words he had used with Elena. Toward the end he spent hours sitting by himself, in the patio of a house that his friends had lent him, in the district of Azul, just thinking, drinking *mate* and looking out over the plains.

"He had met her in that very same place. After traveling around and around the Province of Buenos Aires, he ended up right back where he had started. Macedonio fell in love with Elena before he met her, as he used to say, because they had told him so much about her that it was as if a spirit had come to visit him. Even many of the things he had done earlier in life were to impress her at a distance and to try to get her to fall in love with him, he would say. He always thought that his passion is what made her ill, he always thought it was his fault that she died. Macedonio saw her for the first time at a cousin's house the day she turned eighteen, and again by coincidence one afternoon on a street in Azul. This second meeting proved to be definitive. He had gotten off the train because he was doing an experiment having to do with measuring the length of thoughts. He got off there without knowing where he was because he had already traveled the number of leagues needed for his thoughts, and had decided to send a telegram from there saying he would be coming back late. When he left the post office he sat down at a bar to have a brandy, and then walked around the corner and ran into Elena, who was looking at the window of a shoe store, as if she had been placed there just so Macedonio would find her. She started to laugh because she thought it was funny to see that man dressed in a white shirt and a dark suit at siesta time, as if he were sleepwalking in a lost town in the middle of the Pampas. He looked like a seminarist going out to ask for alms for the poor of the parish. And I was asking for alms, Macedonio would say, because she gave me the grace of her beauty and of her intelligence, bright as the morning sun. He invited her to have tea with him at the café in the train station, and from that afternoon on, they were together until the day she died."

"Elena saw her death coming. Even though no one was able to find a single symptom of any known illness, even though Macedonio Fernández was really the one who was perpetually ill, and who tried extravagant systems of gaucho medicine, such as drinking fermented milk and soup, and never took any chemical medicines, and even though he was the one who experimented with medical knowledge, she was the one for whom death was imminent. That is why her illness and Elena's end and Macedonio's attempts at curing her with his medical knowledge were such a tragedy. Macedonio thought Elena's death was an experiment that included his life in the future. A scientist does not personally participate in his experiments, that is what makes him different from a mystic. But Macedonio participated until the very last moment in Elena's illness, trying to cure her. To give you an idea, it would have been as if Einstein had gone personally to Hiroshima to test his theoretical hypotheses on the structure of the atom. When Macedonio finally realized he had been defeated, that life was a horrible erosion destined to kill everyone off one by one, and that he was unable to stop the illness, and that it was even useless for him to try to get sick in her place, he agreed to have her taken to the hospital. He circled about the pavilions and looked through the windows of her room, from the outside, not daring to go in. He went around the gardens and waved at her through the glass, not daring to go in and see her die. From then on he hated all doctors and scorned medicine, which he considered to be a hopeless science, incapable of fulfilling its mission of preventing human beings from dying. Doctors are always failures, it is only a matter of giving them enough time. They have never been able to save anyone from death. They are arrogant imbeciles, precisely because they have never succeeded and have never been able to save anyone. She was lying in a bed in a hospital and Macedonio looked in through the window, and waved at her from the other side, and she smiled back without any strength left.

"And that is how Elena died, frail and delicate as happiness itself.

"The end was so horrible and so interminable that Macedonio remembered everything—the cretonne couches in the waiting room, the physical impossibility of going to the bed where Elena's body lay in pain—with the distinct feeling of being in a dream and being unable to wake up from it. In the waiting room there were other men waiting at sunrise for other agonies to end. They smoked and stared into space in a time without time, where what one waits for is what people who are distanced from the pain refer to in resignation as 'the inevitable.' Until one afternoon her brother Alfredo came down the corridor toward the waiting room, and Macedonio saw his face, which had been his father's face, and gestured for him to stop, and Alfredo leaned against the white tiles of the wall and watched him walk away. He would not be back, let his dear kids grow up as bastards, he wanted to negate everything that would remind him that she had left this world. Elena's death (she was twenty-six years old) was an unexplainable event, it belonged to a parallel universe, it had occurred in a dream. (He dreamt that she was killed in a field of straw by a group of tigers.) As if he had paid a man who was coming down a dirt path in the dark with a lantern and handed him her body for him to hold. In exchange for what? It was a deal. He thought that sacrifices were actions that maintained the order of the universe. They were not public (they had ceased being public), but they still had to be performed, and instead of arrogant theatrical ceremonies they were now being performed on innocent and beautiful victims in white hospital rooms. If this was the case, then there was still hope. The sacrifice had already been consummated and he decided to place himself at the center of an experiment. I was married around that time, and my wife became very good friends with Macedonio—he was polite and courteous with women, a seductive man, friendly, incredibly intelligent, anyone who knew him will tell you that. A first-class intelligence, he would discern paradoxes instantly, tautologies, I remember that one of the first things he said to me was that he was interested in William James because James studied beliefs. Philosophers, he says to me, are generally interested in tautologies (in other words, in mathematics and formal logic), or in proofs (events and verifications), but not in absent reality. I can still hear him, that soft firm voice of his.

" 'Absence is a material reality, like a hole in the middle of the grass.'

"After Elena's death, he could not go on living, and yet he did go on living. (*Io non mori e non rimasi vivo,* is how Dante cried.) He told me that he remembered a Russian student who had had a bomb blow up on his body because he had not wanted to kill an innocent family that was crossing the street (the mother, the children, the French governess) when he was about to carry out an assassination attempt on the chief of police in Odessa. He met him in Adrogué, years later, old and completely disfigured by the explosion. He was like a ghost. When a man loses the woman he loves he is like the man who has a bomb blow up on his body and does not die. That is why Macedonio thought that the impetuous Rajzarov was like his brother, that Russian who was made more of metal than life. His steel teeth sparkled when he spoke, he had a silver plate in his head, a gold lattice interwoven like a three-dimensional tattoo held together the few strands of cartilage and bone that were left in his right knee—a man-made badge of pain that he would always recall simultaneously as a painful memory and as a circle of liberating fire, as a medal of honor that he carried about with the utmost pride. For it was invisible, recorded inside his body. An operation in the dark that lasted four hours, on the Eastern front, in a basement of the organization in Crimea, they did not have any sulphamide, or any anesthesia, no wonder he was so proud. That is how Macedonio had ended up, metallic, impaired, held together by operations and prostheses, the same pain and the same body arti-ficially reconstructed, because Elena was suddenly absent. Frozen, made out of aluminum, walking as if his arms and legs did not be-long to his body, like a metal doll, he was unable to smile, he could not raise his voice. 'There is nothing left that does not hurt.' "

"His friend Rajzarov was with him when Elena died, he spent the entire day with him, walking about with the heavy melancholic movements of a robot, the weight of iron in his soul, the absence stamped on his chest. Macedonio was lying on a couch and the daunt-less Rajzarov tried to cheer him up a bit. Macedonio listened very attentively to his anarchist exploits, without saying a word. But once, after a pause, when Rajzarov was taking a break, drinking a brandy, Macedonio said in a voice that seemed weightless from not having spoken in hours:

" 'An Austrian general once said to my father: "I will think of you after I am dead." For me to think about her is normal, but for her to think about me, now that she is dead, is something that saddens me deeply?'

"He could not handle the idea that she, dead, might remember him and feel sad because he was alone. He was thinking about the memories that survive after the body is gone, about the white nodes that stay alive even when the flesh disintegrates. Engraved on the bones of the skull, the invisible forms of the language of love stay alive. And perhaps it was possible to reconstruct them, to bring those memories back to life, like someone plucking music written in the air by a guitar. That afternoon he came up with the idea of entering those remembrances and staying there, in her memory. Because the machine is Elena's *memory,* it is the story that always returns, eternally, like the river. She was his Beatrice, his universe, the spheres of hell and the epiphanies of heaven. There is a heretical version of the *Divine Comedy* in which Virgil builds a live replica of Beatrice for Dante. An artificial woman that he finds at the end of the poem. Dante believes the invention and destroys the cantos he has written. He looks for Virgil to help him, but Virgil is no longer at his side. The work therefore becomes the automaton that allows him to recuperate the eternal woman. In that sense, I have been his Virgil. Months and months locked up in the workshop, reconstructing the voice of memory, the stories of the past, seeking to restore the frail form of a lost language. Now they say that they have deactivated her, but I know that is not possible. She is eternal and will always be eternal and in the present. To deactivate her they would have to destroy the world, negate this conversation and the conversations of those who want to destroy her. She is like the river, flowing slowly and calmly in the afternoon. Even if you are not in it, the river still flows. They will not be able to stop something that began before they understood what was happening.

"I am Emil Russian," he said. "They think that I have a replica, but I am not the one who has a replica, there are other replicas, she produces stories, indefinitely, stories that become invisible memories that everyone believes are their own—those are the replicas. This conversation, for example. Your visit to the Majestic, the woman who drinks indefinitely from a bottle of perfume, the young woman in jail. You do not have to leave the island, this story can end right here. Reality is endless, it is transformed and becomes an eternal story, where everything always starts again. She is the only one who remains still, always herself, motionless in the present, lost in memory. If there is a crime, then that is it. She has no images left, there are only words in her memory, the peaceful flapping of the birds, the voices at night. I will show you the Archives, you will be able to see for yourself that the story is infinite. Look," he said, and turned on a screen on the wall. An old super-8 film came on. At first a few numbers appeared on top of some moving lines, then the picture began with an old man, with white hair, wearing an overcoat, coming out of a wooden house, walking across a garden and sitting on a wicker chair and smiling.

"That man, the one you see right there, was a poet, a philosopher, and an inventor."

Sitting on the wicker chair, Macedonio looked at the camera and lifted the lapels of his overcoat, as if trying to stay warm, while he said hello with a slight nod of his head.

2

They have closed down the Museum, so it is necessary to get past the iron fence that separates it from the street to get in. If one goes across the gardens, one can see a small light glowing in a window on the ground floor. To get there you must go up a ramp and through the circular rooms, until you reach the central gallery. The machine is at the end of a white pavilion, held up by a metallic frame. Her octagonal shape is somewhat flattened, her small legs resting on the floor. A blue eye pulsates in the dim room, its light breaking the stillness of the afternoon. Outside, on the other side of the windows, it is possible to hear the low rumbling of the cars heading west down Av. Rivadavia. The motionless machine blinks repeatedly in an irregular rhythm. At night, the eye glows, all alone, and its reflection shines on the window.

Are you Richter? Is somebody there? Of course it can't be Richter. I just said that because I was afraid. As long as you're there, I don't care who it is. And if there is no one there? And if I were alone? No one comes anymore. It's been days and days since anyone has come. An empty, circular place with windows facing the gardens and a stone ledge, on a platform, where I have been abandoned. Does anybody care what I say? Mental loneliness. Loneliness is a mental illness. They have locked up, no one can come here anymore, no one has ever come. Sometimes I have hallucinations, I go back over the archives and look for words, everything is so slow that I can barely see the light in the window, across the hall, I picture Fuyita in the lower level, sitting in his rocking chair, keeping watch, I can't quite understand it, could they have left me alone? To disappear? I know there is a camera recording me, the eye of a camera in the corner of the ceiling, I can picture Fuyita in the small room below, his multiple vision of the entire Museum on the small closed-circuit screens, we are all going to end up like that, one machine keeping watch over another, the small video cameras on the corners of the ceilings, held up by mechanical arms, turning like glass eyes, sweeping and recording the rooms and the galleries. Sometimes they also record Fuyita's memories, leaning on his walking stick, making his rounds through the Museum, wearing his municipal guard uniform and carrying a flashlight to see the corners and the stairwells. His small image, distorted in the empty space, and then Fuyita sitting on the rocking chair, again in the level below, rewinding the tape to see himself walking through the galleries. This Museum has become the biggest of its kind in the country, dedicated to the art of surveillance, just machines keeping watch and a guard going over the rooms. I know the Police Museum, with the wax reproductions of the criminals. Punk Head, Madman Gaitán, Ángel the Bad Boy, Agatha Galifi, Ranko Kozu, life-size, wearing the clothes they had on when they were arrested or killed (the shirt with the bullet hole in back), and the cells where they were locked up by the Argentine justice system, and the instruments used by the police for centuries to hold the murderers. He used to say to me that narrative is an art that belongs to the police, that they are always trying to get people to tell their secrets, to narc on other suspects, to tell on their friends, their brothers. That is why the police and the so-called justice have done more for the progress of narrative, he used to say, than any writer in history. And I? I am the one who narrates. For hours on end my image is the only thing that can be seen in the level below, it is actually recorded by two cameras, one in that corner over there and the other in that other corner on the ceiling. They only see my body, no one can get inside me, the brain's loneliness is immune to electronic surveillance, television screens only reflect the thoughts of those watching them. You can only film and transmit the thoughts of people who voluntarily agree to watch what they think. That is what they call daily television programming, a general map of the mental state. The interior monologue, he would say, is now the daily programming on the TV screens, fragmented time, streams of consciousness, verbal images. But they have not yet been able to devise a machine that is sensitive enough to have telepathic television. They are researching it in Osaka, in Japan, Fuyita says, in the secret facilities of Sony-Hitachi, where they run experiments using the brains of dolphins, they want to design a machine capable of reading people's minds and projecting it on a screen. I am an anachronism, so much of an anachronism that they have buried me in this white basement. That is why they want to keep me isolated, under control, under the exclusive surveillance of Fuyita, the Korean guard, like an embalmed corpse. I am picturing the corridors now, the ramp, the inner galleries of the Archives, if I try to remember and the purity of memory does not blind me, then I can see the door of a room, partially ajar, a crack in the darkness, a silhouette in the window. Just the door, partially ajar, of a room in a boardinghouse, was is it fifteen, or sixteen years ago? There is never a first time in memory, it is only in life that the future is uncertain, in memory the pain always returns in precisely the same manner, rushing to the present, you have to avoid certain places as you go over the past with the eye of the camera, whoever looks at himself on such a screen loses all hope. I can see the small lake under the low fog, the gray sky of morning, that is where my father killed himself, I saw the white marsh with the frost around the edges, between the rushes, right next to the mud with the tracks of the feet of the tero-birds. Every story is a detective story, he used to say. Murderers are the only ones who have something to tell, personal stories always turn out to be the story of a crime. Raskol-nikov, he would say, Erdosain, Scharlach the Dandy. My father killed a man as he was coming out of a party. I am sure I will not be able to sleep now, I dream of a Hungarian engineer hidden in a house out in the country, in the skeletal frame of what is left of a ranch where a mechanical bird nests. The party had gone on until dawn and on the way out there was some kind of altercation on the veranda behind the house. I was unconscious for nearly two hours, according to the Hitachi watch that belonged to Fuyita's mother. Then I saw the bright dial again and felt something heavy on my thigh. The Sony plays nighttime music on the radio station, if only I could make contact, transmit. Once a friend's son hung himself so he would not have to serve in the military. He was twenty years old, he was to go to Campo de Mayo, he spent the night before he was supposed to report for service with a woman, then he went back home and killed himself in the tool shed behind their house. Didn't want anything to do with the Argentine Army. Once a friend's daughter received a letter that she herself had written to her ex-husband, who lived in Barcelona. The address had changed, or she had written it down wrong, in any case the letter was returned to sender and she read what she had written six months before. It was as if a stranger had written her a letter telling her the secrets of her life in Buenos Aires. Not at all as she remembered. In the Police Museum there was a room dedicated to the life of Lugones, the chief of police, whose name was the same as his father's, Leopoldo Lugones. He founded the Special Division and introduced a substantial improvement to the torture techniques utilized in Argentina: he took the electric prod, which was traditionally used with cows to direct the cattle up the short ramps and into the English trains, and used it on the naked bodies of the shackled anarchists from whom he wanted to get information. Chief of police Lugones, the son of the poet, was the director of State intelligence, and it was he who carried out his father's work to its full culmination, he was his executor and in charge of writing introductions for all of the poet's poetic and literary compositions. When he used a tool from our cattle industry to improve State control over rebels and foreigners, he advanced and deepened the national spirit in the same manner as his father had when he wrote his "Ode to the Cattle and the Grain." The retired chief of police ended up locked up in his own house in the neighborhood of Flores, with Parkinson's disease, unable to sleep, with insomnia, terrified by possible terrorist attacks, by the possible vengeance of the children of the tortured anarchists, locked up in his own house, with doors and windows barred and an incredible and complex system of mirrors that allowed him to keep watch on all the rooms in the house simultaneously. They were reflected on the slanted mirrors mounted on the ceilings and the doors so he could see the entire house, as well as the garden and the front door, in a single view from a wheelchair on which he wheeled himself through the rooms of the house. This is historically accurate, absolutely historically accurate, it is all in the Police Museum and was also told to me by his daughter, who remembered her father with hatred and sarcasm, locked up in successive padded rooms, keeping watch over the corners of the house with angled mirrors, always armed in case of a possible attack, while he dedicated what was left of his life to protecting and publishing the work of his father, the poet Leopoldo Lugones. And, to assure the accuracy of his father's work, he initiated lawsuits against anyone who alluded to his father's writings without citing the appropriate detective interpretations of his son and executor, who looked over each and every one of the editions of Lugones's complete works, which were read in schools and prisons. At the end, he finally killed himself, Lugones, the ex–chief of police, shot himself with a shotgun, the trigger, and this is known for certain, pulled with his toe, as is the tradition in these kinds of suicides, in these suicide stories the person committing suicide with a shotgun always pulls the trigger tortuously with the big toe, barefoot, while he holds the barrel of the gun aimed at his face. But in the case of Leopoldo Lugones (Jr.), the Parkinson's disease complicated the maneuver to such an extent that the shot went slightly astray and the bullet went through his throat, and it took ten hours for him to bleed to death. In the gallery of the Police Museum dedicated to his memory, on Calle Defensa in Buenos Aires, you can see photographs and other belongings of his, and even his incredible and complex surveillance system, which he designed to protect his life from terrorist attacks, have been reproduced. Macedonio considered him a son worthy of his father, the most worthy son of his main enemy, since the chief of police, following the poet Lugones's strict orders, had Macedonio Fernández followed and watched by the police for all those years, purely out of literary jealousy, envious of the respect that Macedonio's sober attitude elicited among the younger generation, who scorned Lugones for exemplifying the writer who always allows himself to be used by government and those in power. So Macedonio was accused, and with good reason, of being anti-Argentine and an anarchist, and they started following him, which was a worthless infamy, because he was a peaceful man, he wouldn't even kill a fly. At the end even Lugones was being watched by his son's police force, driving him to commit suicide, because the son had threatened the father with denouncing him publicly when his investigations revealed to him that the poet was in an adulterous relationship with a teacher to whom he sent mystical and pornographic letters, with semen and blood splattered on the paper, and when the chief of police, Macedonio used to say, ordered him to leave his clandestine lover and threatened him with making the affair a public scandal, which would destroy his reputation of being a moral Argentine citizen and a representative of the extreme right of Argentina, the poet, with a final gesture of dignity, took a motor launch up the Tigre to a resort and committed suicide in 1938, exactly thirty years before his son would do the same. All of this is in the Police Museum, even the letters written by Lugones's lover, the mirrors of the chief of police, Leopoldo Lugones Jr., and his father's complete works edited and introduced by him with his detective-fiction interpretations, all of that can be found in the Museum on Calle Defensa. Macedonio used to get melancholy when he told the story, but also sarcastic, because he thought that it was a good example of detective fiction on the part of his private enemy, the poet Leopoldo Lugones. That is the first case of a poet whose son was a policeman, it's common to find examples of policemen whose sons are poets, Macedonio used to say, but the other way around is very rare. Was it he who used to say it to me? Did he say it to me just now? Sometimes I get confused and think that I'm in the hospital. I think and I think and I see a corridor, in my memory, and then another, they were rolling me away and I could see the lights on the ceiling and the white-tiled walls. He never thought that he would leave and that I would remain behind here, lost, a woman on a hospital bed, tied down with rubber belts to the back of the bed, my wrists above my head, tied up like that. You're crazy, he said to me, lost, that's the murmuring of love, the voice of the woman who narrates what she has seen, the screen white as a sheet, if I stop then life too will stop, I see what I say, now he's there, right there, he tells me what I want to hear. I am and have been what I am, a crazy Argentine woman who has been left alone, now, abandoned forever, he is how many years old now? They say that his hair turned white overnight when I left, he was always beautiful, he looked like Paul Valéry, more distinguished than Valéry, a real Argentine native, his body smooth, and that way of leaning against me, still talking, whispering on my neck. Once, on the low wall behind my sister's house, during siesta time, he held me like this, with his arm, just like this, he lifted one of my legs and took it out, the buttoned fly, he had been playing paddleball and had that smell and looked straight at me as he put it in me like this, yes, right there, yes, almost sitting on the wall, I wasn't wearing anything underneath, I never wore anything underneath, I felt the skirt against my buttocks, the crease, I was always hot, first he put his open hand right there, as if he were going to sit me in the air, he lifted me up, I was lifted up, there was always a flame burning in the room on Calle Olazábal, against the full-body mirror, you could really see yourself in that one, he had me turn around, my elbows against the wall, until my face touched the mirror, like a cat. We spent a winter in Mar del Plata because he was running away, he'd been found out and was being followed, and they lent us that apartment in an empty building, on Calle Olazábal, you could see the ocean from the small window in the kitchen, and the stove on, above the oven, was the only light at dusk. I am Amalia, if you hurry me I will say that I am Molly, I am her, locked up in the big house, desperate, pursued by Rosas's *mazorca,* I am Irish, I will say then, I am her and I am also the others, I was the others, I am Hipólita, the gimp, the little cripple, I tottered slightly when I walked, Hipólita, I say to him, and he smiles, Hipólita, with "the gloves on her small hands," she ran away with the psychopath, the big castrated psychopath who could tell the future on Tarot cards, he had a scar in his groin from here to here, Fuyita has a slash between his legs, below his torso, like the edge of his hand, a scar, red, an impotent director, the great seducer was all tongue, he carried a stalk of corn covered in Vaseline in his small suitcase, I am Temple Drake and then, oh you despicable creatures, you made me live with a justice of the peace. These and other stories, I have told them already, it does not matter who is talking. I remember, when Richter was around and Perón fell in the German trap and poured everything into trying to build an atom bomb in Argentina and achieving economic independence, during those months of waiting and denial, Evita slapping the ministers around, yes, she would slap the Minister of the Interior on the face the moment he uttered even the slightest derogatory comment about the working classes, about those poor dregs, slap, slap, across one cheek and the other, with her strong little hand, thin and fierce, sometimes she had to just about get up on the toes of her feet because those political bosses were tall, some were dark, but all were psychopaths, they stole everything, even the small lightbulbs from the bathrooms in the government buildings, their fingers yellowed from nicotine, wearing horseshoe tiepins or sometimes the Peronist emblem in diamonds, Eva saw the social injustice cropping up in the ministers themselves and defended herself by slapping their faces, she would call the ministers over and stand up on the toes of her feet and slap them across the face, slap, slap, that is how the Peronist Resistance began. Those stories have circulated from the beginning, from mouth to mouth, when they emptied out her body and embalmed her, that is how she ended up the same, a doll with a small watch on her wrist, so thin that the band was too big and could not be closed, locked up in a box, on top of a wardrobe in the offices of the General Labor Confederation, covered with a blanket, because the marines wanted to throw her into the river, sink her to the bottom. A woman who was not allowed to die in peace, she's also in a museum, God only knows what she was dreaming about when she died. I remember the room in the hospital, all the poor who came to see me, they would stand at the foot of the bed, holding their caps in their hands, they have come to give me their condolences, none of my old acquaintances have recognized me, the Russian is here, Rajzarov came at the last moment, with his metal body, rebuilt, politics is the art of dying, a cold politics of pride, Rajzarov says, of the kind that goes around at night to vindicate the humble and the sad, it is the art of death. The women knitted sweaters for the soldiers in the Plaza de la República. To be anonymous politics must be clandestine, there is a slight breeze coming from the galleries, I'm in a glass room, exhibited like a doll, I'm the queen bee, mounted on the velvet cushion, the tiepin has a pearl and pierces the butterfly's body, you have to pierce them onto the cushion when they are alive, he says, this way they won't end up rigid and they'll preserve their elegance, if you pierce them onto the cushion when they are dead the colors of the wings fade. That's me, the cat strolling through the hallways, alone in this empty room, then left to the inner patio and the window facing the vacant lot. A Korean man, Tank Fuyita, has been the keeper and the guard for years, he came with the second generation of immigrants, smugglers of cheap watches on the free market, they wore the watches on their arms, ten or twelve Japanese watches, and spoke in their Oriental whispers, in the Once neighborhood, in Ciudadela, but liberalism ruined the business, free trade was the end of our smuggling operations, Fuyita would say, the end of Argentine history. That was a river novel, it started in 1776, on both shores of the Río de la Plata, the boat with the English goods, and now it has ended, so many deaths for nothing, so much pain. And now who's there? Fuyita? The Russian? No, who would come around here at this time of day, you're crazy, what are you waiting for, you're dying of cancer, you're just another crazy woman, a crazy nobody waiting at the edge of death. Now I feel like there's a current blowing, the soft flash of lightning in my vertebrae, the electric shock that used to make my sister María turn white with fear. A fine sheer net of incredible exhaustion falls with the edge of night, a fatigue that won't let me think, that's how she used to speak. They kept her in Santa Isabel for almost ten years, they would partially erase from her memory the voices that she tended to hear at dawn, the cadence of the water from the faucet in the bathroom, Sister María used to speak with Satan, she and he had been lovers, she left everything and entered a convent in Córdoba, the Discalced Carmelites, she had sung tango in the Chantecler Cabaret, Sister Ada Eva María Phalcon, they called her The Egyptian, she had been kept by faros and by Argentine gentlemen of the oldest stock who, at the end, when she entered the convent, would travel all night, those men, to hear her sing in the choir of a church. She used to say: "We see the ashes of the days that have gone, floating in the past, as we see the dust of our journeys at the end of the road." That's how she used to speak. She had a daughter with aphasia and educated her with music, a plaintive love song by Esnaola, this is how you strum the guitar, see, you're left-handed so we'll have to change the strings around. She would go out dressed like a country girl, flowered skirt and braids, with her silly old guitar and sing the tango "Sin palabras." Without words, this music is going to hurt you, the girl thinks, doesn't speak, a verbal music, the story of Venus's ring, the daughter sitting in the garden out back. At first it was the sad and small country hotels, the dresser with the mirror above it, and up above, on the shelf, between the hangers, the bottle of perfume, a room facing Av. de Mayo in the Hotel Majestic. They spent two years running from the police, she never knew exactly why, something having to do with morphine, they had rented a coupé, they were singing artistes, on tour, until she decided to stay in Córdoba and enter the convent. She went to the church one afternoon and laid face down on the freezing tiles in front of the altar and opened her arms to form a cross. Sister Superior, she said, I am Ada Eva María Phalcon. Could I join this congregation? I have been evil, I have sinned, the lower I sank the purer my voice became, the more men I slept with the purer my voice was, Sister Superior. I have brought, she said opening her jewelry case, these jewels are for the Lord to use, for Christian charity, for the forsaken children, and she cut her long hair with a pair of shearing scissors and said that at night, sometimes, in the middle of the night, on tour, in the small country hotels, she had heard the voice of Satan, his song, he murmurs music to me vocally, I can't hear him, I have never heard him, I only listen to him, Mother Superior, Sister Clara, Sister. She left her jewelry case at the altar and laid face down until they allowed her to enter the convent (because she was a sinner), and now she sings in the choir with the other nuns, and the men who used to hear her sing in the Chantecler Cabaret now come on Sundays, they travel to Córdoba just knowing, they say, that Ada Phalcon is singing there, lost and anonymous in that choir of nuns. That is a story, in the Archives, that is the story of the singer, there are others, I close my eyes and see, a street, oh, how real, the light on me, the light of day, the pure physicality of experience, the level of the river going down in that house out in the Tigre. I know I have been abandoned here, deaf and blind and half immortal, if I could only die or see him one more time or really go insane, sometimes I imagine that he is going to come back, and sometimes I imagine that I will be able to get him out of me, stop being this foreign memory. Endless, I create memories, but nothing else, I am full of stories, I cannot stop, the patrol cars control the city and the locales below Av. Nueve de Julio have been abandoned, we have to get out, go across, find Grete Müller, who is looking at the enlarged photographs of the shapes etched on the shells of the turtles, I have seen them and now they emanate from me, I pull events out of live memories, the light of the real quivers, weakly, I am the singer, the one who sings, I am on the sand, near the bay, I can still remember the old lost voices where the water laps ashore, I am alone in the sun, no one comes near me, no one comes, but I will go on, the desert is before me, the stones calcined by the sun, sometimes I have to drag myself, but I will go on, to the edge of the water, I will, yes.

Afterword

Ricardo Piglia

Translated by Sergio Waisman

I have always liked novels that have several juxtaposed story lines. This intersection of plots correlates with a very strong image that I have of reality. In this sense, *The Absent City* is very much like life. I sometimes have the physical sensation that one goes in and out of plotlines, that throughout the day, as one circulates with friends, with the people one loves, and even with strangers, an exchange of stories occurs, a system akin to doors that one can open to enter into another plot—something like a verbal net in which we live—and that the central quality of narrative is this flow, this apparent fleeing movement toward another story line. I have tried to narrate this feeling, and I believe it is the origin of *The Absent City*.

The first problem I faced was how to incorporate the stories of the machine. This raised an issue that has always interested me in the organization of a novel: the idea of interruption as a central factor in the art of narrative. As I thought about interruptions, I had in mind certain references, such as Scheherazade, and a series of texts within this tradition, until we arrive at a novel by Italo Calvino that drew my attention, *If on a Winter's Night a Traveler*. That is, a tradition that conceives of the novel as a genre founded on interruptions, and which, taking this as its point of departure, establishes a connection with what one might call the experience of life—which is basically one of interruption and suspension.

Another text that I very much admire, in this regard, is Borges's "Tlön, Uqbar, Orbis Tertius." It is written in a supercondensed manner, within a labyrinthine system, where there is always a corner that pulls you toward another story line. I liked this idea of a plot that is like a street in which you open a door and suddenly your life is completely different. It is from there, perhaps, that my decision came of using the city as a metaphor for the space of the novel.

An additional problem in which I was interested was the idea of imprinting a certain velocity in the narration, a concern no doubt related to the manner in which the transitions between the stories are produced, as well as to the issue of interruptions, fragmentation, and suspense. This idea of velocity was something new for me with respect to my previous books. What I try to work with in *The Absent City* is a degree of extreme condensation and speed while dispensing as much as possible with the recourse of irony, which is a trait that comes naturally for me (it is the defining mark of the writing of *Artificial Respiration,* for example).

A few words, now, about Macedonio Fernández, and some parallels with Joyce. In a way, a formula like the title "The Absent City" is the most Macedonian aspect of the novel. What I mean is that it alludes, even if it is not immediately obvious, to one of Macedonio's fundamental ideas: that which is absent from reality is that which is truly important. This idea expresses his nonpragmatic ethics, which I believe are very appropriate for our time.

The idea of a man in love who walks through a city that belongs to him, but where the city in which he walked with the woman he loved is lost. Because the city is a memory machine. Of course, that lost or absent city also includes other moments of life, not just those associated with a woman. This is how Joyce's Dublin works, for example.

Dublin and Buenos Aires share the fact that they are both literary cities, in the sense that they have had a large density of writers (in the 1930s and 1940s, Macedonio, Borges, Arlt, Cortázar, among others, all lived in Buenos Aires), who have had a tense relationship with the Metropolis. For example, the tension Stephen Dedalus feels with English, which he considers to be an imperial tongue. Similarly, the issue of the inheritance of the Spanish language and the struggle to become independent from Spain was very much present in Argentina. One can see an analogy between Joyce's relationship with Shakespeare, and Macedonio's with Cervantes. The question becomes: whose language is it? And: how do we overcome the political control associated with this language to reach Shakespeare, for example, thinking of Joyce's parodies in *Ulysses,* and the position that Macedonio takes with respect to Spain's Golden Age?

Another point in common between Joyce and Macedonio is a certain hermetism as a poetics. Joyce, the writer who writes so as not to be understood by his contemporaries, who postulates a kind of narrative, and a kind of usage of language, which assumes a distance with respect to any possible transparency of the reading of his work by his peers. It becomes an element of his poetics. The artist who does not seek to be understood by his contemporaries, but rather to present them with an enigma. As Joyce himself said: "I've put in so many enigmas and puzzles that it will keep the professors busy for centuries arguing over what I meant, and that's the only way of insuring one's immortality."

There is something of this in Macedonio as well. But Macedonio takes a position that, in my opinion, is more radical than Joyce's. For although Joyce spends seventeen years with *Finnegans Wake,* at the end he publishes it. Whereas Macedonio spends nearly forty-five years writing the *Museum of the Novel of the Eternal One,* and dies without publishing it.

Both are writers who refuse to compromise with society. One could think of writers who negotiate with society, who establish multiple relationships, and there are certainly some great writers who fall into this category. Then there are those who sever such relationships. Joyce and Macedonio have something of the figure of the writer who makes these ruptures, and then establishes very strange relationships in their place: the scenes of Joyce with the women who maintain him, or Macedonio surrounded by his friends.

Macedonio is also an example of great clarity with regard to the distinction between the production and the circulation of literary material. He understood the two fields very well, spoke elegantly about their division, and constructed a theory of the passage between them (which is, in reality, a theory of the novel). He wrote his entire life, and his books are full of prologues and warnings to the reader and advertisements and opinions about his books, but in real life we could say that he refused to publish. I like this example of a writer who places himself outside circulation, who works in peace, following his own rhythm. The writer who does not conceive of his books in terms of the customer whose order must be satisfied, but rather in terms of the reader who is always looking for a lost text amid the crowded shelves of a bookstore.

Usually, one tends to infer the kind of society implicit from a text, what the society in which it was written must have been like. What I have tried to do with "The Island," instead, is create a society that might constitute the context for *Finnegans Wake*. Not the society within which Joyce wrote the *Wake,* which would point to Ireland in tension with England, and everything else that makes up the context of the real text. But rather: what would be the imaginary context in which the *Wake* could function? Or: in what society would *Finnegans Wake* be read as a realist work? The answer is a society in which language is constantly changing. This approach has interested me for a long time as a possible model of literary criticism. I believe literary criticism should try to imagine the implied, fictional context of works of literature. In this case, the question became: what is the reality implicit in *Finnegans Wake*? And the answer: a reality in which people believe that language is that which is written in the text.

The same thing could be said about *The Absent City.* You could say that *The Absent City* is a novel in which I imagine a society controlled by stories, that it is like a realist novel of a society in which what really exists is spoken stories, machines that tell fragmented, Argentine stories. There you would have a connection between what I do with *Finnegans Wake* in "The Island" and what is supposed to take place throughout *The Absent City*.

With certain contemporary writers, such as Thomas Pynchon and Don DeLillo, I feel I have something in common that I refer to, somewhat in jest, as a fiction of paranoia. In a way, it derives from other readings, such as William Burroughs or Philip K. Dick, or Roberto Arlt. It is the idea of a conspiracy, which is very much present in these writers, and in *The Absent City* as well. The idea that society is constructed by a conspiracy, and that there is a counter-conspiracy in turn. This pulls toward a certain kind of relationship with genres, and toward a reflection of politics as intrigue. I do not mean political literature in the traditional sense, in which there is a private and a public world, with the political novel more closely linked to the public one. But rather the manner by which politics is present in literature when these two categories have dissolved—and perhaps this, then, would be the definition of the postmodern, the dissolution of the tension between the public and the private, and the dissolution of the tension between high and low culture. So that when these oppositions have dissolved, the conspiracy, the intrigue, appears as the model that the subject holds of what politics is in society.

The private subject perceives the world of politics almost like the Greeks conceived of destiny, or of their gods: as a strange manipulative movement. This is the perception that some novelists, including myself, have of the world of politics. That is, politics enters the contemporary novel through the model of a conspiracy, through the narration of an intrigue—even if this conspiracy is devoid of any explicitly political characteristics. The form itself constitutes the politicizing of the novel. The conspiracy does not necessarily have to contain elements of a political intrigue (although it may, as is the case with Norman Mailer) for the mechanism of utilizing a conspiracy to be political. It can be a conspiracy involving the delivery of mail, or a conspiracy involving Italian immigrants in Argentina, or any other invention. It is the form itself that illustrates the fictional perception of politics in our world today.

This idea, parenthetically, is already present in Borges. He was the first to use this formula, because "Tlön, Uqbar, Orbis Tertius" is based on a conspiracy, as is "Theme of the Traitor and the Hero," and "The Garden of Forking Paths," among others. So that Borges, with his miniaturization, was the first to speak of parallel worlds and of conspiracies as paranoid political representations of reality.

This perception of a relationship between things that are otherwise incompatible is an important aspect of contemporary fiction. A subject who obsesses deliriously with history, or a subject in delirium about a universe—or, in *The Absent City,* for example, subjects who experience deliriums about realities that are not as they appear to be.

Finally, I believe that the translator experiences a very strange relationship with the author of a book. The issue is not just questions associated with style, references, possible mistakes, or what kind of modifications can be established in the translation of a text. The interesting thing, rather, is the kind of work involved in translation—for it seems to be an unusual exercise in relation to reading, on the one hand, and to property, on the other. I have always been interested in the relationship that exists between translation and property, since the translator rewrites an entire text that is his/hers, and yet is not. The translator finds him/herself in a strange place, in the sense that what he/she does is transpose into another language a kind of experience that both belongs to him/her, and does not. A writer cites from another's text, or simply copies, as we all do sometimes—because one forgets, or because one likes it too much not to do so—but the translator carries out an exercise that draws a path between both places. Translation is a strange exercise of appropriation.

I hold the same relationship with literary property as I do with property in society: I am against it. I think there is a game with property in translation. That is, it puts into question something that common literary sense takes for granted, which is the fact that issues of property in literature are extremely complex, just as they are in society. Language is a common property; in language there is no such thing as private property. We writers try to place marks to see if we can detain its flow. There is no private property in language; language is a circulation with a common flow. Literature disrupts that flow, and perhaps that is precisely what literature is.

Ricardo Piglia was born in Adrogué, in the Province of Buenos Aires, Argentina, in 1940. He is the author of numerous short stories, novels, and critical articles. His books of fiction include *Jaulario* (1967); *Nombre falso* (1975), translated as *Assumed Name* (1995); *Prisión perpetua* (1988); *Respiración artificial* (1980), translated as *Artificial Respiration* (1994); *La ciudad ausente* (1992); and *Plata quemada* (1997), which received the Premio Planeta.

Sergio Waisman is Assistant Professor of Spanish and Portuguese at San Diego State University. His translation of Ricardo Piglia's *Assumed Name* received a Meritorious Award in the 1995 Eugene M. Kayden Translation Contest.

Library of Congress Cataloging-in-Publication Data
Piglia, Ricardo. [Ciudad ausente. English]
The absent city / Ricardo Piglia ; translated by
Sergio Gabriel Waisman.
ISBN 0-8223-2557-8 (cloth : alk. paper)
ISBN 0-8223-2586-1 (pbk. : alk. paper)
1. Waisman, Sergio Gabriel.   I. Title.
PQ7798.26.I4 C5813 2000863'.64—dc21   00-029392

Made in the USA
Middletown, DE
01 April 2019